# LAST STAGE WEST

## Frank Bonham

Chivers Press • G.K. Hall & Co.
Bath, England • Thorndike, Maine USA

This Large Print edition is published by Chivers Press, England, and by G.K. Hall & Co., USA.

Published in 2000 in the U.K. by arrangement with Golden West Literary Agency.

Published in 2000 in the U.S. by arrangement with Golden West Literary Agency.

U.K. Hardcover   ISBN 0-7540-4127-1   (Chivers Large Print)
U.K. Softcover   ISBN 0-7540-4128-X   (Camden Large Print)
U.S. Softcover   ISBN 0-7838-9013-3   (Nightingale Series Edition)

The text of this Large Print edition is unabridged.
Other aspects of the book may vary from the original edition.

Set in 16 pt. New Times Roman.

Printed in Great Britain on acid-free paper.

**British Library Cataloguing in Publication Data available**

**Library of Congress Cataloging-in-Publication Data**

Bonham, Frank.
  Last stage West / Frank Bonham.
  p.      cm.
  ISBN 0-7838-9013-3 (lg. print : sc : alk. paper)
  1. Large type books.   I. Title.
PS3503.O4315 L3      2000
813'.54—dc21                                    99–462295

LT-W

# CHAPTER ONE

## *1861*

*Burnsville, Mo., July 11:* A locomotive and four cars of the Missouri & Arkansas Rail Road were derailed three miles north of here last night. Railroad officials said the fireman received serious steam burns from which he is not expected to recover.

According to Peter Canty, an investigator for the railroad, the wreck was caused by a stump which had been placed on the tracks by disgruntled farmers who recently lost a lawsuit against the company.

Mr. Canty states further that fifty thousand dollars in state currency, consigned to a bank in Burnsville, was stolen from the train. He emphasizes, however, that as the currency was unsigned it will be of no value to the thieves. A state banking official was to have signed the banknotes after the safe arrival of the money in Burnsville.

Mr. Canty declares that an arrest may be expected momentarily.

(From the *St. Louis Courier*)

Harry Logan was working in the harness room of the Overland Mail Company when the big man named Pete Canty stopped outside the door and peered into the dusk of the small room. Working at the bench among scraps of leather, Logan tried not to seem aware of him. In the month since Canty had taken over the investigation of the train wreck, Logan had come to despise the man and his manner of questioning. There was an arrogance about him; at first it was a sort of jeering civility, but now that he had failed to accomplish anything, the iron corners of something more brutal had begun to tear through.

Canty entered and drifted over to the bench where Logan was putting an edge on a skiving knife. Logan felt his temper whetting itself like a cat sharpening its claws. He pushed it down, knowing he could not afford to lose his temper with this man. Without looking up, he said, 'Howdy.'

'Hello,' said Canty, in his slow, mocking way. He chewed a matchstick as he leaned against the bench. He wore a black corduroy coat, black trousers, and a flat-crowned black hat. His dark face was dented with small scars like the pits of birdshot in hardwood. He stood there watching but saying nothing. Finally Harry's gaze flicked up at him.

'If you want to ask me something,' he told him shortly, 'you'd better get to it. I get off at four today.'

'McCloskey said you were leaving early,' said Canty. He shifted his weight, causing the bench to stir and Logan to make a false cut in the leather. 'Going for a ride into the country, I hear.'

'Where'd you hear that?'

'McCloskey said you'd begged the use of a company wagon. Now you know you didn't need a wagon to drive two blocks to call on the Harper girl. So you must be driving her out to the farm.'

Logan laid down the knife. He was a long-boned, solid man with threads of lines at the corners of his eyes. 'How can a man as smart as you waste a month trying to find out who laid a stump on the railroad tracks?' he asked, with a faint jeer in his voice.

'Oh, it's easy!' replied Canty. 'You just go by the rule book. Give all the suspects a chance to make a damned fool out of you. Hell, you could spend the rest of your life on the job.'

'What else can you go by, except the rule book? You can't lock up the Harpers just because a train was wrecked on a farm they used to own. Or me because I know old man Harper's stepdaughter.'

Canty crossed his arms, his big hands massaging his biceps through the heavy brown stuff of his sleeves. 'When I lock you up,' he said, 'it won't be because you know somebody's stepdaughter. You've got more reason to be mixed up in it than any four suspects I could name. Who had his two-bit stage line cancelled out when the railroad came through? Who landed on the Overland Mail payroll, shovelling manure and making harness?'

'Do you want an answer to that?' Harry said.

'Don't bother. I know more about you than you know yourself. I know you had a brawl one night with some railroad men over a threat you made to wreck our trains. All I don't know is why I didn't lock you up when I first hit town. In some places that'd be evidence enough to hang a man.'

'Is it evidence when it isn't true? I said the railroad had so many enemies it was just a question of time till your trains started getting derailed. And the next night somebody wrecked one. Well, what did you expect? The state handed your company more land scrip for building the road than there were public lands to cover. So you took the farms along the right-of-way. Were you waiting for them to thank you?'

'I don't make the rules,' Canty said. 'But I'm sure as hell going to start enforcing them.'

'If you enforce them any more than you have been, they'll lock you up for assault and battery.'

Canty chuckled. 'Not in this town. Folks around here are beginning to get the shakes. Nearly everybody in Burnsville subscribed

4

some money to get the bank started last year. And now it's got the weak trembles. Depositors are needing money, and there's not much left to give them. The railroad's had to dump in some more cash to protect its own deposits. And it's still trembling.'

Harry began to slice the thick leather to a feather edge. 'The paper said the bank's in good shape,' he argued.

Canty suddenly snatched the knife from his hand and said sharply, 'I'm talking to you mister.' He shoved the spade-shaped blade against Harry's throat, and Harry tilted his head back quickly and hit Canty's wrist so that the knife flashed across the room. He was so close to smashing the man on the jaw that his shoulder muscles groaned for release. Surprise opened Canty's dark, cynical eyes; then fury spread over his face, and moving back he drew the revolver at his hip and the tip of it looked squarely at Harry's belt buckle. For that instant there was no doubt at all in Harry's mind that he was going to fire. Then Canty's eyes looked tired, and he said, 'I could blow you apart, Logan, and nobody'd ever touch me. You'd better savvy up to that. There was some talk about lynching you one night—did you know that? But I saved you. "Leave him to me," I said.'

Harry's heart was still pounding. 'Thanks,' he said. 'What do I owe you?'

'You owe me some straight talk,' said Canty,

5

as he slipped the Colt away. 'That's why I made them wait. You're no use to me dead, but you're going to start being some use to me alive. You're going to tell how you and the Harpers went about derailing that train and stealing fifty thousand dollars. I reckoned you might tell me accidentally. Now I'm waiting for you to tell me on purpose.'

Harry picked up the knife while Canty watched. He moved behind the bench. 'I told you before: I was right here when the train was wrecked.'

'The hell with where you were when it happened; I'm talking about *before* it happened—when the stump was laid on the tracks.'

'Same answer. I was right here.'

'How do you know where you were if you don't know when it was put there?'

'I'm here all the time.' Harry shrugged.

'What about the money you withdrew from the bank the day before the wreck?'

Harry's gaze faltered, and Canty said quickly, 'You thought I didn't know about that, eh? You thought Canty didn't know you were packing twelve hundred dollars in a money belt.' With the back of his hand he struck the belt under Harry's shirt. 'Where'd it come from, Logan?'

'From the stock and equipment I sold when I closed out.'

'Why'd you take it out of the bank?'

6

'I was going into business with it.'

Canty leaned on the bench, crowding his face close to Harry's, giving him no time to think. 'Then why didn't you?'

'Because the wreck messed up my plans.'

'*How* did it mess up your plans?'

It sounded feeble, Harry realized; it sounded made-up. But it was all true. 'I was going to California to start a stage line,' he said. 'But after the wreck I didn't want to leave the Harper girl alone till it was cleared up. And I thought it might have looked bad for me, too, leaving all of a sudden.'

'So it might,' sighed Canty. 'So it might . . . How's the reading and writing going?' he asked suddenly. 'I hear your school-teacher lady friend has kicked you all the way up to McGuffey's Third Reader.'

'Eighth,' said Harry.

'Just for practice,' grinned Canty, 'read this.' He pulled a slip of paper from his pocket and smoothed it on the bench. A pulse throbbed in Harry's head and he knew that now he was going to get the real reason for Canty's visit. He was not raking over the same coals. Something had happened. Harry could not make out much of the scrawled pencilling, and the detective explained: 'It's a telegram from up the line. It says Fred Harper was picked up trying to pass some of that currency in Quincy this morning. So you might as well start talking.'

There had never been much question in Harry's mind about the Harpers' part in the wreck. Luther, Bill, and Fred Harper were the shiftless sons of a no-good old whisky-fighting farmer. They had worked the land lackadaisically enough until they lost it to the railroad. They had then settled down to spread their grievances thin enough to cover all their faults. The only Harper he cared anything about was Kelsey, who was a Harper solely by virtue of her mother's second marriage. But he cared a great deal about her; so that now, looking at the message, he was anxious about where Fred's arrest left her, not to mention himself.

'The Harpers are trash.' Harry shrugged. 'But what's this got to do with me?'

'I'm glad you say they're trash,' Canty said, 'because it sort of makes me feel better about what I've got to do.'

'What've you got to do?'

Sucking a tooth, Canty gazed out into the yard. 'Well, like they say, if you can't play by somebody else's rules, write your own.'

Harry came around the bench as Canty sauntered to the door. 'Stay away from the girl,' he warned.

Canty turned with a wicked mirth in his eyes. 'Why, you just told me the Harpers are trash, didn't you?'

'She's no more a Harper than you are! She hasn't lived out there since her mother died.

That's been two years. Leave her alone.'

'Oh, I wouldn't hurt her,' said Canty with that dark strain of sarcasm in his voice. 'Well, I might have to jostle her up a bit, but not so's it'd mark her up. That's just common sense.'

'I'll tell you what else is common sense—that if you put a hand on Kelsey Harper, there won't be a square inch of Pete Canty without a bruise on it.' Harry was suddenly talking hard and fast.

Canty inspected him with indolent contempt. 'If I decide to make her talk, how are you going to stop me?'

'Try it, and I'll show you.'

'That sounds like a pretty good arrangement. Let's see—she boards with the Cogginses, don't she? I'll run on over. See you later.'

Canty stepped into the yard and Harry moved into the doorway and caught his arm. Canty turned like a big, lithe cat. His eyes were looking at Harry's chin as if he had picked out the spot he was going to hit. When Harry tried to raise his arms to defend himself, his elbows collided with the frame of the door, and he realized Canty had done this many a time, that it was brawler's strategy to hamstring a man while he chopped him down. The railroad man's fist was coming in and Harry winced and turned his head. The blow landed on the side of his jaw. He reeled into the room. Canty followed and pushed a short, hard jab into his

9

belly and caught him on the mouth as he doubled over and sat down.

Canty was standing over him, turning a craggy silver ring on his finger. 'You better work up to the ninth reader before you tackle Canty again, Logan. The next time I hit you, the face on this ring is going to be lookin' at you. And I'll keep on hittin' a while before I cool you.'

Out in the hot afternoon, some hostlers had run up. In Harry's gaze their faces, like Canty's, had a soapy, out-of-focus look.

'Now that you and me have got straightened out on things,' said Canty, 'I'll tell you a secret: I'm giving the girl overnight before I go to work on her. First I'm going to talk to Luther and Bill and their old man. Then her card comes up. And she's going to tell me what happened out there that afternoon, if I haven't already got it out of them. Because I know she was there, and if she didn't help you, she at least knows where the rest of the money is.'

Canty rolled his shoulders like a hawk settling its feathers, and Harry began to understand how murder grew out of hatred.

'You see, it's a kind of pushin' contest,' Canty explained. 'The bank keeps pushin' the railroad to find that money, and the railroad pushes me. So I've got to push somebody too. Now that I know for sure it's the Harpers I want, and probably you, I ain't about to lay around till snow flies getting my hands on

10

those banknotes. You just tell Miss Kelsey that when you see her, eh? And then ask yourself if maybe you ought to talk first.'

## CHAPTER TWO

Exactly at four Harry finished his work and left the harness shed. He went to the small room the company let him occupy and sat on his cot with his back against the wall, smoking a pipe while he thought of what Canty had said, had done, and might do. He thought of leaving tonight, taking Kelsey with him. But that was, no doubt, exactly what Canty wanted them to do.

He was sick of this town and the people in it. It had been a good town where everybody knew everybody else and wasn't afraid of him, suspicious of him, above or below him. Then the east-west Overland Mail pushed through and it began to change; the railroad snaked down from the north and in a few months you'd never have known Burnsville. Two or three men bought up most of the land the railroad had taken from the farmers; and they, the new merchants, and some others bought control of the bank. It began to matter how much money you had. The doctor, preacher and school-teacher descended to their rightful rungs farther down the social ladder, being

11

people who knew much about life, death and learning, but mighty little about making money.

And then the train wreck occurred and some big people were awfully close to becoming little. Until his talk with Canty, Harry Logan had not been aware how shaky things were with the bank. It explained the nervousness he had sensed since the robbery.

Suddenly he got up and knocked his pipe out on the doorframe. You couldn't believe a thing Canty said, and he might be with Kelsey right now. But badge or not, there would be no rough handling when he questioned her. She would be home from the school by now and ready to drive out to the farm to pick up some odds and ends which had belonged to her mother.

Harry had an old pistol he used to carry on the stage sometimes. He got it out of his trunk, but then shook his head and replaced it under some clothing. If he carried it, he might be tempted to let it do his thinking for him. He was close enough to trouble right now without shooting someone.

He closed the door and crossed the stage yard to a gate in the rear. Inside a second yard were grain sheds, some green and yellow company wagons backed up to a wall and sheltered by a shake roof, and a quantity of equipment too old to use and too new to throw away. Harry had taken a breast collar and started for the corral when Superintendent McCloskey's voice called him.

'Logan. Come here.'

McCloskey was standing near a feed shed with a rolled newspaper in his hand, swatting his leg with it. He was a big, middle-aged, waddling man with sloping shoulders and the manner of an overseer on a plantation. He stood there hitting the paper against his leg until Harry walked up.

Harry looked at him and waited, saying nothing, but thinking, 'You ignorant cabbage head. How did you ever get this job? On my worst day, I could run this station better than you'll ever run it.' McCloskey had a country haircut, a country manner, liquor blotches on his face, but enough money in the bank so that in the new Burnsville many people called him Mister.

'What happened to those bags of grain?' McCloskey snapped.

Harry glanced beyond him into the dark dustiness of the shed. 'Nothing, as far as I know.'

'Rats have tore half the sacks open.'

'Some people think cats are a good idea where there's rats,' Harry mentioned.

McCloskey hit his leg again with the paper. 'Some people think they're a bad idea where there's horses. Take a look at the damage in there.'

Harry was on the threshold when he smelled

13

tobacco and heard a little grunt of exertion, and knew there were men in the shed. But when he tried to back out, McCloskey's fist hit him in the back of the neck and he fell forward. Then from the darkness men were swarming over him; he was kicked several times before two men seized his arms, hauled him up and rammed him back against the wall. He threshed and kicked, but someone came forward with a pitchfork and the tines popped through his shirt and stabbed his belly lightly. He held his breath and looked at the man who held the fork. It was George Bliss, one of the big farmers.

'Did you say something?' Bliss asked, with a grin that was a shine of teeth in the dark. He was a big, rugged man with broad shoulders. A horseshoe of black hair lay upon his brown bald head.

'It was rats all right,' panted Harry. 'The kind cats are no cure for.'

A man shouldered in and slugged at his head. Harry kicked him in the shin and the man swore and said, 'Let him go! Give him to me!' He didn't sound very anxious about it. He was a corpulent man with a face like a pit bull and the disposition of a terrier. This was Jesse Arnold who managed the Burnsville terminus for the railroad company.

'Hackles down, Jesse,' said George Bliss. 'Got the rope, Ed?'

McCloskey, holding a coil of half-inch

14

manilla, said, 'Ee-yap!'

For an instant Harry choked on a fear of that rope. He had seen men hung; seen their faces blacken and their tongues protrude and their necks pull long and thin like toffee. But he did not truly think they were ready for lynching. Otherwise they'd have waited for dark. After dark the mildest men got brave; and some of the men in here were pretty mild—Gene Buckley, the merchant, and two others who worked in the coal yard.

'I guess you talked to Canty this afternoon,' said Harry.

'I guess we have,' said big George Bliss.

'Then you ought to know about Fred Harper.'

'We know about Fred, and we're making a good estimate about you. Where's the rest of the money, Logan? What was your cut? It ain't in your room, because we've looked there. Where'd you bury it?'

'I was working right here when it happened. I haven't been out of town since.'

'How do I know you were here?' demanded McCloskey. 'You were supposed to be cooling-out a team. How do I know you finished the job?'

'I wasn't the only man in the yard. Ask the others.'

'I have,' said the superintendent. 'There ain't a one of them'll testify for sure to where you were at.'

'They scare easy,' said Harry. 'Got a living to make.'

'But you haven't,' cut in Bliss. 'You've got a bale of my money and these other boys' waiting for you. Is the Harper woman keeping it for you?'

'The Harper woman—' Harry began. And then something comic about this businessman's lynch mob caused him to smile. Trying with scowls and numbers to be tough. Canty was tougher in the lobe of his ear than they were anywhere. 'I've talked enough today,' he said. 'Anything you want to know, ask Canty.'

They were silent, momentarily baffled. 'All right, Ed,' said Bliss grimly.

McCloskey stepped up and dropped the noose over Harry's head. Harry spat in his face. The superintendent gasped, wiped his face, and gave him the palm and then the back of his hand. The men began shoving him around. Suddenly the rope grew tight and Harry made a strangling sound and tried to reach up to loosen it. But now several of the men were hauling on it, and the ones who were not got into the spirit and joined them. Harry fell to his knees, and they began hauling him through the door and into the yard. Grunting and panting, they skidded him around. His hands reached the rope, but he could not loosen it until they stopped dragging him. Then he tore it loose at once and got up as

16

they came towards him. There was a mattock leaning against a wall, and Harry swung it over his head like an executioner's axe and waited. They halted.

'Come on,' Harry invited. 'You'll never get better odds.' His chin was scratched and bleeding and the rope had burned his neck. He was still gasping.

'You're asking for trouble,' said Bliss presently.

'I've got trouble. Come on and I'll share it with you.'

McCloskey blurted suddenly, 'You're fired! Pack your stuff and get out.'

Harry grinned. 'Oh, I thought I was going to be made assistant. You sure do need assistance, Mr. McCloskey. If you were freezing to death, I'll bet you couldn't chop down a warm tree.'

Some of the men smiled. McCloskey wasn't the best liked man in town. But George Bliss spoke sharply. 'That's enough, Logan. If we'd meant to string you up, don't think we'd back down so easy. This was meant for a warning. We've got Fred Harper, but we want the money too. We're giving you until tomorrow night to lead us to it, in case Fred don't talk. The next time we come we'll mean business. Come on, boys,' he said.

McCloskey, the last to leave, said sourly, 'You'd better not leave the station. Canty wants to know where you are. By God, if you

17

think we're bluffing . . .'


## CHAPTER THREE

'People don't leave you much when they start talking do they?' the girl said to Harry. She was slender and ash-blonde with dark-lashed grey eyes and a pretty but sober mouth.

'Not in this town,' agreed Logan.

'They didn't even leave me my name. Everyone used to call me Kelsey. Now I'm "the Harper woman"—half sister to the Harper gang. Everybody is sure the boys got that money, and just as certain that I got part of it. Why, that man Canty looks at me as though stolen notes were falling out of my sleeves.'

Harry had not told her yet about his talk with Canty. He had cleaned up after his battle with McCloskey and his friends, and the only marks were some scratches on his chin and a rope burn around his neck, which didn't show with his collar buttoned. He had been afraid the super would withdraw his permission to use the wagon, but either he forgot Harry was using it, or Canty wanted to see where he went with it.

They reached the eastern end of town. Harry turned the team north across the tracks. Beyond the small brick station were rolling fields and nubby green hills, and here and there, like gunny-sacking thrown upon the hillsides, the dun of ploughed earth. Except for a few old buildings, Burnsville was only two years old. The town was thought promising, nourished as it was by the Butterfield Overland Mail, which started at Tipton and went twisting like a vine through the south-west until it reached San Francisco. The richest sap of this vine was siphoned east and west, but some of it was tapped at the junction towns like Burnsville.

After the short-line railroad came and brought a payroll with it, everyone was happy except a few farmers who had been cleaned out. And of course Harry, whose stage line had been nullified by the railroad.

'Even the children snicker when I write something on the blackboard,' said Kelsey. Harry saw she really had it on her mind. Women were odd creatures: Instead of raising a good healthy anger over such slights, they got hurt. 'Of course it isn't their fault,' she said, 'they're just mimicking their elders. And you can't mend a reputation like a cracked cup. Yesterday Mrs. Coggins asked me to find another place to board. I was glad I could say I was taking a teaching job in Quincy.'

Harry adjusted the lines. 'You know, I'm wondering if Quincy's the place for you after all,' he said.

'Why not, Harry?'

He looked at her. 'They arrested Fred there

this morning. He was trying to pass some of that money.'

'Why—why I don't believe it!'

'Surprised?' Harry smiled.

She glanced down. 'Not so much surprised, I suppose, as startled.'

'I kind of thought you'd be more startled than surprised. So I talked Canty into questioning you tomorrow instead of tonight— to give you time to work up a good case of surprise.'

The clear grey eyes came up again. 'Harry, what *are* you saying?'

'I've been letting you make up your own mind about things,' Harry said. 'But all of a sudden it's got right late in the day. I figure you've got about twelve hours to decide how to tell Canty that you were out here the night of the wreck.'

Colour came up her throat. 'You knew that, and never said anything before?'

'Everybody knows it,' Harry said grimly. 'Mrs. Coggins told somebody you borrowed their buggy to drive out that afternoon.'

'But she knew I only drove out to dig some vegetables. And I gave most of them to her.'

'But the way she's telling it now, you drove back about midnight with the horse all in a lather, and spent the rest of the night walking up and down your room. Listen, Kels,' Harry said earnestly, 'you don't have to sell me on trusting you—but Canty's got a badge. And

20

withholding information is as bad as taking part in a crime. So if you know about how Fred got hold of that money, you'd better tell Canty about it tonight.'

'I—I can't,' she said weakly. 'The boys would go to jail. What they did was terrible— but what the railroad did was worse—robbing all those farmers of their land and buildings. Not that I have any use for Luther and Bill. But I don't want to be the one to send them to jail.'

'What about the wreck? Did you see it happen?'

Her face looked tight-lipped and pale as she gazed down the road into the thickets. 'No. The boys came out a little while after I did. They said they'd come to collect some tools. Just when I was getting ready to leave, I heard the crash. In a little while the boys rode up to the house. I was inside, and they didn't see me. I saw them hiding something, and I went out on the porch. They were angry and scared, but they didn't have time to move it, because people were coming up the hill with lanterns to get tools to move the wreckage.'

'Where did they hide it?'

'In the well. They pulled out some stones and made a place behind them.'

'I wonder if they went back and moved it,' Harry said.

'I don't know. I should think they'd have been afraid the farm was being watched. They probably kept some of it, and that was what Fred was trying to spend. What can I do?' she asked Harry anxiously. 'If I do go to Canty now he'll make trouble for me.'

'If you don't, you'll go to jail. I reckon Canty will settle for your testimony and leave you alone. Let's go back. The furniture will keep.'

Kelsey shook her head. 'I'll talk to him tomorrow. Maybe Fred will tell on the others first; or Canty will get it out of them, now that Fred's in jail. If he hasn't found out by tomorrow morning, I'll tell him.'

Up ahead, Harry saw where the turning to the farm cut across the steel slash of the rails. 'I wish your mother'd never got mixed up with this outfit,' he growled.

'*You* wish it!' said the girl. 'She only married Harper so we could be together after my father died. But it was worse then because Harper was so slothful, and the boys took to pestering me. So I had to board out and start teaching when I was fifteen. And we weren't together anyway.'

Harry took her hand. 'Forget you ever heard of them. After you wind things up with the railroad, you and I are getting out of here. I've had all I want of working for a big company. I could run this agency better than McCloskey and never take a deep breath.'

The girl's face was troubled. She looked at him. 'What would you do if you quit? All you know is staging, and it seems to be all railroads these days. The papers are full of them.'

'Not the California papers.' Harry tried to hold down the exhilaration he had kept bottled up all summer. 'One of the drivers was reading me a thing from a Sacramento paper a while back. It seems there isn't a stage line in the gold country that runs on schedule. And I said to myself right then: That's for Logan. I'm going to have my own line.'

Kelsey frowned. 'But it would take a fortune. A coach alone would exhaust most of your capital. And there'd be salaries and feed and rent—'

Harry shrugged. 'Oh, I'd need a loan. But credit's easy on the coast.' Yet his confidence had begun to melt like a candle in the sun because he knew exactly what came next.

'Is credit easy,' Kelsey asked, 'for a man who doesn't read very well?'

'Look at it this way,' Harry said. 'I expect to have the smartest wife in California. That ought to make some difference, oughtn't it?'

Kelsey touched the deep amber calluses on his palm. *'That's* the hand they'll loan the money to, Harry—not mine. If that hand can't make the letters properly, they'll laugh you right out of the bank.'

Harry pulled back his hand. Like the miraculous gas-bag at a county fair, he had floated high; but the cool air of reason had started him down again. He felt annoyed and a bit sunk, knowing how much a man was handicapped whose fingers tapped along under the lines of a page like a blindman's cane.

'Well, I could get a grind organ and a monkey, I reckon,' he said gruffly.

'Harry Logan,' Kelsey said, 'one of these days you'll be the biggest man in staging. But that will be after you learn your Three R's. It may take some time. That doesn't matter. What does matter is that you keep at it—as a man with a wife and children has no chance to.'

Harry looked into her grey eyes, full of warmth, and suddenly felt sure of something: She loved him. He stopped the wagon, put his foot on the reins, and turned to her. She let his arms go about her. She let him kiss her. But in the midst of it, he learned something else: Life had handled her so roughly that she had learned how to keep her head and heart from confusing one another. She took part in the kiss just enough to let him know she enjoyed it too; but hardly what a man would call recklessly.

'Some day, Harry,' she sighed, 'it will be so wonderful that we'll forget how long we've waited. And there will be furniture in our home—and children who aren't wearing hand-me-downs. And there will be love in my eyes when I look at you—not desperation. Go to California, Harry. Get started—and then see how fast I come when you send for me!'

'All right,' he said firmly. 'I'll dicker with you. We'll wait, providing you come to California and teach school until I'm making good. Otherwise I'll go to St. Louis tomorrow and spend all my money on girls with sequined skirts.'

'Well, I certainly won't have *that*,' she declared. 'So as soon as things are set right here, I'll go out too.'

Harry kissed her again and they drove on. He felt fine now, sure of himself and where he was going. In his mind he had stored more facts about managing a stage company than Superintendent McCloskey would learn if he hung around stagehorses until he began to whinny. Harry was like a clever mechanic who had saved the best of a hundred machines he had junked until he was ready to build one better than all the others. And now it was time to head west and put his own machine together . . . if Canty and some men with a rope would let him.

# CHAPTER FOUR

After leaving the stage yard, Pete Canty strolled down to the Choctaw Saloon, where old man Joe Harper lay around. His zest in manhandling Harry Logan had already soured in him. These days satisfaction was a fire of wet wood which he had to nurse along with similar small pleasures which helped him to forget that he was being made a damned fool of by somebody in this town. He had a good job with the railroad and he wanted to keep it. Sometimes he was sent ahead of the engineers to help some property holder decide to sell his right-of-way for a sensible price. Other times he would help move a farmer who was putting up a fuss over being evicted by the railroad. But he wouldn't have his job five minutes after the bank failed.

Before entering the saloon, he reread the telegram. At last he knew for sure it was the Harper gang that had wrecked the train. But the telegram also informed him that Fred Harper had been caught with only the banknote he had been trying to pass, so they still did not know where the fifty thousand dollars was. And Canty knew enough about courts of law to predict that Fred might even weasel out of jail on some yarn about getting the stolen note in change.

He crumpled the telegram, jammed it in his pocket and butted the saloon doors open with his knee. He saw Joe Harper drinking beer at a table with some friends. He was a big old fellow with a blotched face in which the liquor he had been blotting up all his life had settled until his features looked like those of a drowned man's. It was a face Canty

26

particularly despised because it reminded him of his father's. His father had run various small drinking places where Canty had learned the smell, taste, feel and look of humanity in its most naked moments, when the ratchet in the roller broke and the shade went flying up on the small, private rooms of the soul. Canty was old friends with viciousness, cheapness and despair. From childhood, he had been holder of the gigantic secrets that virtue was merely vice with its collar turned backward, and that an honest person was one who thought you were watching him. All this knowledge had hammered him into the shape of a knife—keen, surprisingly honest, at times bitterly cruel.

Canty dropped his hat on Harper's table and sat down. He made a gesture towards Harper's companions as if he were whisking flies from the table. The men shrugged and moved away.

'Your son, Fred, is in jail,' announced Canty.

'What for?' asked Harper, leaning back. Across his groin, like a sling, passed a wide brown belt to support his belly, in addition to the heavy belt which supported his trousers.

'For passing some of the money he and the others stole off that train. They picked him up in Quincy . . . Fred writes a mighty poor hand, don't he?'

Harper was so full of beer that he seemed only half awake. He frowned muddily, tipped his face down and pressed his fingers against his cheeks as if they burned and he was cooling them. 'Own damn fault,' he muttered. 'His sister's a teacher.'

'I'm talking about him and his brothers. You can make it easier on them, old man. Tell me where the rest of that money is. If I get it today, I'll ask the law to go easy on 'em.'

'When'll you see Fred?'

'Tomorrow.'

Harper's bloodshot eyes opened. 'Tell him he can rot in hell for all I care. Them thieving off-scrapings sold my last crop and kept the money. There's no damned honesty in the world any more. You can't trust Injuns, you can't trust lawyers, you can't trust your own sons.'

Canty grinned. 'You've been a long time finding that out, friend. I'll tell you something else you ought to know: If I find that money on your land, you'll go to jail too.'

'Get fed in jail, don't you?' countered Harper.

'Slop.'

'What do you think they feed me here? I'm the swamper.'

'I could get you a job with the railroad,' said Canty, trying to smile but with an expression as of bile in his mouth. 'Easy work. Sweep out the station. Carry in stove wood.'

'So help me God,' snarled Harper, 'I'd sooner go to jail. Roust a man off his land like a boar-hog—then offer him a job to keep him from starving!'

Canty rubbed his jaw. 'Hell, nobody cares if you starve. I'm just making you a deal to save the good name of the Harpers.'

Harper leaned aside and spat on the floor. 'Looky,' he said, 'I'm glad they got the money. I hope it wrecks the bank and the railroad. And I hope the tramps end up in drunkard's graves.'

'It's not likely,' said Canty mildly. 'Takes time to die of drink. Lute and Bill don't have that kind of time.'

'Don't fret me about them, then. They hang round the Junction House. Talk to them.'

'I aim to.' Rising, the railroad man took a card from his pocket and frowned at it. 'Well, your stepdaughter's next. Pretty little thing. She bruise easy?'

'The hell with her too,' scoffed Harper. 'Has she raised a hand to help me since I lost my land?'

'Where I come from,' said Canty, 'only one kind of a man would let a woman support him anyway.'

As he walked off, old man Harper hit him in the back with his beer glass. Canty arched his back. Then he turned and walked back. His movements were consciously slow, as if he enjoyed feeling the muscles work. Harper's eyes tilted up at him, bloodshot and savage.

'You old pig,' said Canty through his teeth.

He pushed Harper in the face and the old

29

man fell back with a yelp. Canty looked at him as he wallowed like a downed cow. There was something particularly nasty about a man who could say of his own sons, *To hell with them*. It was too much like home, to Canty.

He stood under the wooden awning, gazing up the road towards the railroad station. He took a match from the ribbon of his wide flat hat and chewed it slowly. A wagon was crossing the tracks and starting north on the old mail road. Logan and the girl. He meant to let them get out of sight before he followed.

Just as he was starting for the livery stable where the company horses were kept, he saw two men leave the Junction House Saloon near the railroad station. One was tall and yellow-haired; the other was short and swung his hands the full width of the walk as he strode from the saloon. They were Luther and Bill Harper. They ducked under a hitchrack and mounted horses. At a jog, they started up the road after Logan and the girl.

Canty hesitated an instant. He decided to take a handcar. At the depot he picked up two guards who were off duty. These days the railroad company had to maintain guards to keep disgruntled farmers from tearing up the tracks. They set a handcar on the rails, laid rifles and manacles on it, and started for the Harper farm.

'What's up?' asked one of the men. He was a rough-looking, red-bearded man with hands

30

like mallets.

'That's what we're going to find out. It looks like three men and a girl have gone out to dig up some money.'

'The girl too, eh? Really think she helped dump that train over?'

'Why not?'

'Don't look like the sort for it. Purty little thing . . .'

In his dark face, Canty's teeth gleamed in a smile. 'Let's have a couple of verses of *Mother*, eh, Rube?' He winked at the other guards. 'Listen, Red, ninety per cent of the trouble in the world starts with some purty little thing eggin' a man into something. The other ten per cent starts with the man eggin' her into something. Now, lay on that bar, dammit. We haven't got all day.'

## CHAPTER FIVE

In the warm, late afternoon, Luther and Bill Harper tied their ponies in a plum thicket. They had been smoking to keep the gnats at bay, but now Luther grunted, 'Knock out your pipe. They might see the smoke.'

Standing at the edge of the thicket, he regarded the small cabin farther up the ridge on which he and Bill now stood. An hour ago the railroad telegraphist had come to the

Junction House Saloon and blurted the news about Fred to the whole saloon. Luther had been startled: He had not known Fred had held out any of the banknotes when they hid them. A few minutes later, when he saw Harry Logan and Kelsey leaving town, he realized he and Bill had to get to work.

'See 'em, Lute?' asked Bill tensely. A slope-shouldered man of middle height, he wore frowsy black whiskers on his chin and jaws. Long ago a misfire in blasting stumps had knocked out four of Bill Harper's front teeth and obliterated some fine but important print in his mind.

'No. Reckon they're inside. I see the wagon, though.' Lute Harper was a tall, dishevelled looking man with an everlasting expression of annoyance. His fair hair was long, his upper lip was thickened on one side. Despite his sleepy look, he was quick-minded and restless.

'You reckon she told Logan?' asked Bill.

'Don't matter now if she did. We've got to move that stuff. We could have left it there till it was safe to use it, but Fred's spoiled *that* caper.'

'Then whatta we gonna do?' As Lute started up the ridge towards the cabin and barn, Bill trailed him closely.

'We'll have to move the money. Then we'll take off—move away for a year or so. When it's safe we'll come back, collect the money and start spending it in the big towns and cities.

We'll get hold of some honest-to-God currency and copy off the treasurer's signature on to ours. It ain't counterfeit, so how are they going to catch us? Lots of ways we can change it into coin if we take our time.'

'What if Logan tries to stop us from moving it?'

'Don't worry about *that* long-shanked hoss-handler. He makes a better fist at shovellin' corrals than he'll make in a scrap. I never did have any use for him; but after he swindled his sister out of her share of the stage line that finished him with me.'

'He do that?'

'What do you think? Think he sent his sister the money in St. Louis after he sold out?' Lute didn't know; he just figured Logan would have kept it, because it was the logical thing to do. He backed his hatreds with bitter, unsubstantial arguments. He had fought men because they were bigger than he. He hated Pete Canty for the tiny bluish pockmarks on his face. He hated his father for his swinish habits, though they were only Luther's habits grown old. And he despised Harry Logan because he had once inherited a stage and some stock.

They reached the back of the barn and scrutinized the unkempt farmyard—a toppled woodpile, a broken well-ring, and an apple tree pulled down with its weight of yellow fruit.

'Where they at?' whispered Bill.

33

'In the house. Logan just passed the door.' Lute hefted his long, homemade rifle. He wasn't anxious to have a murder charge against him, but he'd kill Harry if he had to. 'He ain't so tough,' he thought, 'a long drink of water like him—hit him in the middle and he'd break like a stick.'

Something else to decide about was Kelsey. The more he figured on it, the more he thought she'd have to go with them. In the first place, it would be smart to cancel her out as a witness to the train robbery. In the second place, someone who wrote a good hand would have to sign those notes. After she'd signed them, she wouldn't be very quick about coming back to Missouri because if any of the stolen money settled out in a bank and they got to studying signatures, Miss Kelsey would land in the ladies' section of stony-lonesome.

'Come on,' whispered Lute suddenly. 'I'll take him first. If I have any trouble, you pitch in.'

Just as they reached the porch, the mosquito bar door opened and Logan stood in the entrance, tall and steady.

'Lose something?' he asked.

'Came mighty close to losin' somethin',' grinned Lute. He swung the rifle to cover him. 'We're comin' in.'

Logan retreated to the center of the room. Lute followed him into the small room with its half-loft and ladder, its atmosphere of rat

34

smell, grease and poverty. Logan stood planted in his strength like a tree, his big hands knotted like ropes, his rawboned face tense.

'Lute, what do you want?' asked Kelsey, from the fireplace. A small fire was smoking; she had been burning papers.

'I want you to stand right there till we're finished. Bill, see to it.' Lute set his rifle near the door, leaned down and rubbed his palms on the dirt floor and then worked them together. 'Shoot him if he goes for a gun.'

'What's it about?' asked Logan. 'Tell us that much.'

'It's about you and her taking what belongs to me and Bill.'

'Lute, that isn't so!' cried Kelsey. 'We came out to get some things of mother's—that's all.'

With a swift motion, Lute made a little run at Logan and started a kick at his groin, but he halted as the other dropped his hands. Lute hurled into Logan's face a handful of earth he had scraped from the floor. Logan put one hand to his eye as he backed away. Lute pulled back his right fist and threw it. Logan ducked it, but Lute caught him with another on his blind side. When Logan shook his head and backed, Bill yelled, 'Git 'em, Lute,' and Kelsey cried at Lute to leave him alone.

Lute went raging into Harry with a roundhouse right hand, but Logan twisted away and Lute missed him. Then the tall man snapped back at him, and Lute had a swift, chilly awareness of the breadth of his shoulders and the craggy look of his fists. Logan thumped him in the chest with a powerful blow, cracked another to Lute's cheekbone, and knocked him sidewise with a swing to the ear. Lute sprawled against the table and fell with it. A load of preserves Kelsey had set out crashed down with him. Dazed, he came to his knees in a shining shrapnel of broken glass, the stinging fragrance of piccalilli relish in his nose.

Logan lunged swiftly around the overturned table as Lute sprang up and seized a chair. He swung it as Logan charged in. Logan halted and the chair legs grazed him. Lute raised the chair over his head, and Logan backed. Bloody faced, Luther stalked Harry until he had him in a corner. Then he smashed the chair down at his head. The chair legs splintered; but Harry had ducked and slipped past Lute. Lute whirled and struck at him as he ran, struck twice more and missed both times. Harry moved around like a twister through a cornfield. Suddenly he seized a chair too and rushed at Lute.

They circled. Logan's face was white, but his eyes were like charcoal smudges. He was stalking Luther now. *That damned fool Bill*, Lute thought. But as Logan backed him through the broken glass on the floor, Lute could hear Bill yelling encouragement like a kid at a street fight.

'Bill!' Lute shouted.

Logan's chair whistled down at his head. Lute parried with his chair but it was driven back in his face. He took a blow in the forehead which stunned him. He felt himself falling, then landed with a grunt on all fours. A pair of wrinkled brown boots moved into his vision and planted themselves there. Now he was going to get it; yet he could not stir. Suddenly the boots twisted and Lute had the impression that the man who wore them was falling. He looked up in time to see Logan coming down with a puzzled scowl on his face. Slack-limbed, Harry Logan fell loosely as Lute wriggled away. Bill stood there with a piece of firewood in his hand.

'Got 'em,' he chortled. Lute scrambled up as Logan was rising groggily on all fours. Then Lute saw Kelsey going for the rifle standing by the door. He yelled a warning at Bill, who darted to catch her as she reached the long rifle. He tore it from her hands and locked his arms around her while she fought.

'Don't you touch him,' she said. 'Take the money and go away—'

Lute waited patiently as Logan forced himself up. On his knees, the man stared dully at Lute. He saw Bill wrestling Kelsey against the wall, and scowled and swayed to his feet and staggered towards him. Lute set himself and cracked his fist against Logan's mouth. Logan staggered away and almost fell. Lute jarred him with another blow to the head. He was suddenly lifted by an exhilaration of pure savagery—a feeling of release as though a sore had been lanced in him. As he hammered at Logan's face with his knuckles he taunted him: 'How do you like them apples, Mr. John Butterfield? Well, let's try it this way—Oh, that 'un hurt, did it? Well, ain't that a pity!' His voice became almost tender, more like that of a cruel man teasing a weeping child than of one man beating another.

At last Logan fell and lay still. One arm sprawled into the rubble of ruined preserves. Lute heard Kelsey weeping, distantly, like someone in a far room.

'Wasting time,' Luther said to Bill. 'Gimme a hand outside.'

In the yard, Bill slid down the well-rope to recover the money. Lute heard stones falling into the water as he worked. A moment after Bill emerged, they heard men working along the railroad tracks. Lute stared at Bill, then down at the tracks. Pete Canty and a red-bearded man came into view carrying rifles. Another man followed shortly. They stopped to peer up at the farmhouse. Canty abruptly hit the other man with his elbow and started running for the farmhouse.

'Git the horses!' Lute snapped. 'Take that box with you! I'll hold 'em off.'

As Lute ran for the cabin, something went by his head with a little *ssst* and crashed into the mossy shake roof. The gun boomed. Lute swerved behind the wagon. Bill gave a sort of bleat and Lute heard the tin box strike the ground. He saw Bill sitting down near the barn, looking fascinatedly at his thigh. Groaning, Lute dug a linen cartridge from his pocket and reloaded. From behind the wagon, he could see Canty running up the road with one of the other men beside him. Bill got to his feet and gingerly tried his leg.

'Git runnin'!' shouted Lute. Bill obediently recovered the money and limped into the barn.

Lute rested the barrel of the rifle on a spoke and sighted on the railroad men. He wanted Canty as a starving dog wanted meat, but the detective kept changing direction, crouching as he ran. Lute decided on the red-bearded guard, who came straight up and down like a tree, deep of chest and blowing like a locomotive. The side-hammer fell, smoke and thunder rolled from under the wagon. Down the hill the guard fell with a meaty thud like a cow going down.

Across Luther's mind ran the thought: *I've killed him!* His heart thumped excitedly in his throat. He reloaded as Canty's shot *whanged* off an iron rim. Lute heard the horses coming. He fired at the thicket where Canty lurked, reloading, and saw the detective's short barrelled rifle fly from his hands as he grasped his wrist. Then Canty dropped back into the brush and Lute heard him retreating towards the railroad.

Bill rode up, leading Lute's horse.

'Can't hardly ride with this leg, Lute,' he complained.

'Hang on. I'll fix you up later.'

*I killed that slob*, thought Lute with a joyful numbness as he strode into the cabin. He prodded Logan with the muzzle of the rifle, wondering whether it would be best to kill him too. Kelsey came at him like a cat. The back of Lute's hand knocked her down. She seized a piece of broken glass, but got tangled in her skirts as she rose. Lute twisted her arm up behind her. She was screaming, her pretty features haggard with hate and fear.

'You've killed him,' she cried.

'No, I ain't,' drawled Luther. 'Looka there, he's bubblin' when he breathes.' Blood was stirring in the corner of Logan's mouth.

They had to tie the girl's hands before she would come with them. Kelsey rode one of the wagon horses, Lute leading it with a come-along. Bill was still fretting about his leg. He was beginning to babble like a child. Lute glanced at the torn and blood-soaked cloth below his hip, and then up at Bill's white face.

'I'll fix you pretty quick,' he grunted. But he knew Bill was bleeding to death.

They reached a brushy trail east of the farm. 'Where are we going, Lute?' asked Kelsey. She had quieted down, trying to out-think him, Lute figured.

'Hard to say. Wherever we go, we're a-travellin' first class.'

'But Bill needs a doctor.'

'Bill's got a doctor. Doctor Lute Harper.'

Another trail beckoned, this one taking them south-west. As it closed about them he felt snug and safe. A man who was ready to kill held all the aces. If he had already killed he had nothing to lose by killing again, but a man who would dance around trying to avoid hurting anyone was plumb asking to be jailed.

They rode until after dark, making twenty miles. A thicket was their camp that night. They had berries to eat and crab apples from an orchard. Bill could not sleep, and towards sunrise he began to rave.

## CHAPTER SIX

It was Pete Canty who hauled Harry back to Burnsville. Harry knew little about how he had travelled from the farm to his small room behind the stage company shops. The doctor who took the workmen's cases told him about it when he changed the dressing on the back of his head the following night.

'Canty lugged you in on a handcar, Logan. You weren't in much better shape than the railroad guard he brought in. Somebody belted you over the head. What happened?'

41

Harry frowned at the ceiling. 'There was a . . . a hell of a fight, I remember.'

'I figured there might have been. What were you fighting over?'

Suddenly Harry struggled up from the cot. 'Kelsey! Where'd she go?'

'We thought maybe you could help us there, Harry. Where *did* she go? Where did any of them go?'

Harry stared around the room, which came in and out of focus like a watery reflection. 'Do you feel like talking to sombody?' asked the doctor. 'Come in, Mr. Canty. I think he's rational now.'

Canty's dark, pitted face floated high above Harry. He heard him speaking to the doctor. 'He wasn't rational when he and the girl tried to ace the others out of their share.'

'You still think they were all in it together?' asked the doctor.

'I'm twice as sure as I was before. I saw Logan and the girl take off for the farm. Then I saw Lute and Bill follow them. Then I find Logan beat up, the girl gone, and an empty cache in the well. Maybe I ain't smart, Doctor—but I can figure that one out.'

Harry heard all this without quite comprehending it. He gazed up at Canty and asked, 'Where'd they go?'

Canty wore a white bandage about one wrist. 'So you and the little lady were just collecting bric-a-brac, eh?' he scoffed. 'But Bill and Luther didn't think so. And now they've all left the table and there you are with just the neck of the chicken—and here I am with a dead guard. Want to help me find the rest of the chicken?'

Harry's thoughts were like a vapor that he tried with his bare hands to compress, but all that came through was that Kelsey was gone.

Canty's voice kept picking at him like a beggar's fingers, but it did not reach the little attic room where Harry's mind was living now.

'I think you'd better try again tomorrow,' said the doctor.

'I think he's a sly dog, that's what,' Canty snapped. He began shaking him by the shoulder. A firefall of pain dazzled Harry. Then there was nothing. When he looked around the room again he was alone.

The next morning as he sat on the edge of the bed with one boot in his hand, wondering whether he could finish dressing, Superintendent McCloskey came in and stood staring at him.

'I hate a rotten loser,' pronounced the superintendent. 'That wasn't a stage line you had, anyhow. It was just a two-wagon livery barn. Shame on you, Logan—big boy like you. Wrecking trains to get even.'

'My wagons ran on time,' said Harry. His lower lip split and began to bleed.

'If mine don't, it's because of lazy hostlers like you.'

43

'I'll be running coaches when you're shovelling out barn stalls,' said Harry.

McCloskey laughed. Harry lurched up from the cot, but his head rocked and he reached for something to steady himself before he slumped back.

'Set down before somebody knocks you down,' advised the superintendent. 'I ain't going to turn you out until you can walk, but I wouldn't want to be standing too close to you when you walk down the street.'

All the rest of that day, Harry tried to get some line of action going which would take him to Kelsey. She and Lute and Bill had gone, and apparently their trail had died among hundreds of veinlike trails through the thickets. Harry would start from the room, weak as skimmed milk, but at the coach barn he would have to stop, the pain behind his eyes stabbing at his brain. Recovering, he would realize there was nowhere to go anyway.

On the fourth morning a dam dissolved in his mind and strength and clearness went flooding through him. Though he felt translucent, like a fingerling trout, he savoured the quickening of his mind and body.

That afternoon he decided to pack and get out. He would rent a horse and try some of the neighbouring towns where Luther might have stopped for food. As he transferred things from his trunk to a valise, he heard the door scrape open. He smelled a cigar, and turned

44

his head to eye Canty standing in the room. The grim black eyes watched him thoughtfully.

'Well, well,' said Canty. 'Joining the army or something?'

'That's it,' Harry grunted.

'Which army?'

'I haven't picked one yet.'

Canty drew a note-case from his coat and handed some flimsy new notes to Harry. Harry silently rose and studied them. He could read the words at the top—*State of Missouri*—and then in a flash he saw a familiar cursive hand at the bottom—finely made letters which he had copied for hours in the evenings.

Canty read from another note: '*"For the Treasurer. A. Baker."* A stands for approximately,' he explained. 'It's Baker's name, but Kelsey Harper signed it for him.'

Harry could imagine her signing, with Luther sitting across a table from her threatening her life if she stopped. 'Are they in jail?' he asked finally.

'Shoot, I thought you were gonna tell me. They bought two tickets for California with this money. The money came back in the pouch last night. Just two tickets; Bill died in the brush.'

'Where did they get on?'

'Martin's Station, day before yesterday. The day before that, a man bought a pen-holder and some pens, an ink-horn, and a new Colt at Syracuse. He said he was joining the Rebels.

45

The money he used came back to the bank here. You'd better get a move on, if you want to catch up with 'em. Stage comes through right soon. Won't be another for three days.'

Harry sat down. 'What are you going to do about it?' he asked Canty.

Canty opened both hands, looked at them and closed them as though he were squeezing rage. 'Damn them both!' he said savagely. 'This is Missouri, and they're already in Arkansas. By the time I reach Arkansas, they'd be in Texas. I ain't needed many women in my time, but I need that one.'

'Why?' asked Harry bluntly.

'Because she's going to be my star witness. She was running the show, or was until you and she got greedy. Somebody had to sign those notes, and it wasn't going to be you or the Harpers. You give me an hour with Miss Kelsey Harper, and I'll have signed statements that'll hang you, jail her, and put that currency back in the bank where it belongs. But now, damn it, she and Lute'll have to be extradited.'

'Extradited?' repeated Harry.

'Meaning they can wreck a train, kill a couple of men and steal fifty thousand dollars, but if they make it across a state line they can thumb their noses at me until I get papers to bring them back.'

Harry said levelly, 'You don't have to extradite a person who wants to come back, do you? I tell you she was kidnapped.'

Canty smiled unpleasantly. 'Well, now, that's possible. Maybe Lute *did* drag her along to sign the notes. And now that it's done, he may have'—hesitating delicately—'disposed of her. Maybe you ought to follow them and see. Are you going to?'

'Yes. Are you going to try to stop me?'

'Oh, I could. But I'm counting on you to kill Lute for me. Beat him to death with a rock; club him with a pistol butt—only make it painful. Then I can sleep again.'

'What's the matter—afraid of him?' Harry countered.

'No, no—I just hate to have my record spoiled.'

'Best way not to spoil your record is not to tackle anybody your own size.'

Canty suddenly thrust the tip of his cigar close to his eye. 'Next time you open your mouth to me, you'll get this right where you can see it best. *You're* my size, Logan. Try me some time.'

Harry turned away and went to one knee beside his trunk again. He hated this arrogant bull of a railroad policeman with a bitterness like gall. He heard Canty breathing through his nose as he watched him pack. 'When you get all packed,' Canty said quietly, 'you and I are going for a walk.'

Harry turned and faced him blankly.

'Down to the jail,' Canty finished. 'Suspicion of murder. For all I know, you may have shot that fellow I had with me the other day. You were up there with the Harpers. Also I want to find out whether that money you're packing started life as unsigned State currency.'

Numbly Harry turned back to the trunk. Out of the corner of his eye he saw the railroad man saunter to the window to gaze out. Harry turned swiftly and caught him on the side of the head with a crashing haymaker. Canty slackened. Harry turned him quickly with one hand and smashed him on the chin. Canty's eyes closed and he frowned like a sleeping man being awakened by pain. Harry hit him once more and let him down. Quickly he looked out the window. In the stage yard, six broad-backed Missouri horses were being groomed. McCloskey was watching the work, his hands in his hip pockets. Harry tied Canty's hands behind him with an old belt, secured his ankles with a cord, and drew his wrists and ankles together. He stuffed a rag in his mouth. Canty's eyes opened and he gazed foggily at Harry.

Harry peered out the window again. McCloskey was complaining about something to one of the grooms. Harry hesitated, staring at Canty. Then he stepped outside, closed the door and walked up to the superintendent.

'Have you got space for me on the stage?' asked Harry.

'We've got nothing *but* space on the westbounds. Leaving us, hey?'

'Yes. Can I have the company rate?'

'The company rate is for company employees. Didn't Pete Canty come out here?' McCloskey asked suspiciously.

'He left ten minutes ago.'

'Told you to leave town, didn't he?'

'He told me I'd better leave before he locked me up. He said he hoped I found Lute Harper and killed him, because he'd never get him back to Missouri anyway. Something about extra—extra-something-or-other.'

'Extradition,' grunted McCloskey. 'All right, I'll get your ticket ready.'

Harry returned to the detective. 'Canty,' he grunted, 'you can blame yourself for this. You made me do it. You'd have charged me with murder. Then when you got your papers—or maybe before—you'd have trailed me, waited till I killed Lute, then brought Kels and me back to stand trial for something we never did. Well, I'm heading west until I catch them. Then I'll head west some more. So don't bother following me.'

Canty's eyes glared with a fierceness which made it plain that nowhere would be too far to follow him.

Harry said, 'Easy now.' He shoved him under the cot. Then he arranged the blankets to cover him from view. He strapped on his gun and was ready.

Presently he saw a few pieces of baggage being carried out. McCloskey stood in the

49

waiting-room, looking disapprovingly at a hunting-case watch. Stage time, Harry concluded. He carried his canvas valise to the baggage room and had it weighed. As he returned, a warm wind brushed his cheek like a child's damp hand, and he looked up. Some weather was making. Well, thunder and lightning would make a fitting exit for the last of the Harper gang.

A watchman, intrigued by sounds in the room Harry Logan had vacated, found Canty that night. He untied him, and Canty's own hands tore at the cord which kept the gag in his mouth.

'Tarnation, Mr. Canty,' the watchman exclaimed. 'Did Logan do that to you?'

Canty wiped his palm across his mouth, spat several times, and started for the door. 'Get out of my way!' he snarled.

He strode through the dark village to the depot. He was with the Burnsville traffic manager for twenty minutes, while the telegraph key babbled messages to and from the home office. At the end of that time Canty yanked the final dispatch from beneath the telegraphist's pencil and read: *Very possible you may be prosecuted. Inexcusable permit Logan escape. Undoubtedly stolen currency went with Logan. Your salary terminated. Expect you in this office tomorrow for full explanation.*

Canty crushed the paper and held it in his doubled fist. The manager retreated as the detective stared at him. Canty was not aware of him. The simple, deceptive man called Harry Logan pulled at his mind like a chunk of iron attracting a compass needle. He started for the door and the manager slipped aside.

'Any—any final message, Mr. Canty?' he asked.

Canty paused with the doorknob in his hand. 'If anybody wants to know,' he said, 'I'm going to follow him.'

'Bring him back, you mean?'

'What's left of him.' Canty said.

## CHAPTER SEVEN

A hard rain broke less than an hour after the stage left Burnsville. Almost immediately the coach slowed, and Harry thought of Pete Canty. Yet if they kept going there was little chance that he could overtake the stage this side of Arkansas. As they forded Brenner Creek, water sloshed in under the doors and the coach tilted. A young woman at Harry's left clutched his arm.

'We're going over!' she gasped.

'Oh, no,' Harry reassured her. 'The worst that can happen is we'll leave the road and travel downstream. In that case you'll have to help us hoist sail.'

She relaxed slowly. As the coach gained the

far bank she glanced at him with a smile. 'You're making fun of me. But we're not used to roads like these in the East.' She was about twenty, her dark hair parted and brushed back and a small bonnet resting on her head. Her face was thin, olive-tinged and very pretty.

At her left, a sturdy, middle-aged man with a bald head like an oak knot turned to glance disapprovingly at Harry. He was tough chinned and abrupt looking, and his thick eyebrows were like caterpillars.

'I was just telling the young lady there's nothing to worry about,' Harry said agreeably. 'I know these roads like the palm of my hand.'

'Is that right?' said the older man. 'I'll stop worrying, then. Since you know the roads.' He turned to watch the dripping greenery move by the window.

The girl pursed her lips, folded her hands and smiled secretly at Harry.

A short time after, the stage horn blew several wet-sounding bleats and the coach swerved in before a small change station. A stinging mist had replaced the rain. The gleaming backs of the horses steamed as the driver and conductor unsnapped the tugs and ran them into the yard. A tall man wearing a grey travelling cape over his shoulders stood in the doorway of the small log building. A little travelling case no larger than a doctor's bag rested at his feet. He stood erect and stern, as if he were reviewing troops. The station

52

keeper was trying single-handedly to walk the new team up to the coach. Harry got out to help him. The man in the cape remained in the shelter as they moved the team up.

'You've done this before,' said the station keeper to Harry.

'I used to help out in Tipton.'

'You wouldn't catch Mr. Fancy Clothes helping, now,' growled the other.

'Is he getting on?'

'Yes—thank God. My good fortune is your bad. I don't know where he came from, but I know where he can go. He rode up with a farmer from Brackenville yesterday. He don't like my cooking; he don't like the cots; well, I don't like him.'

The conductor was talking to the new passenger. He took his ticket and wrote something on the waybill.

'When will we reach Fort Smith?' asked the passenger.

'The schedule says three-thirty in the morning day after tomorrow, Mr. Brown. But I misdoubt it'll be earlier than noon.'

'Hell,' the tall man said. He walked to the stage and got in.

The conductor put his foot on the hub and raised a hand to the station keeper. 'So long, Martin. Don't take any more wooden nickels.'

Harry stared at the agent as he wiped his hands on his trousers. 'Is this Martin's Ferry?'

'Where'd you think you were—Cincinnati?'

grinned Martin.

Numbly, Harry gazed around the rain-darkened yard. 'Then this must be where those train robbers got on.'

'Yep. You know, I thought they were just a honeymoon couple from the back country. And here they were loading me down with bad money.'

Harry wiped the rain from his mouth. 'Did they seem as happy as all that?'

The station tender pursed his lips. 'The man, now, was kind of a hoorawing sort. The girl acted scared, though. But what bride don't? They had a meal with me and she never said one word—You better get on, mister, or you'll have to walk.'

Darkness caught the stage on the winding Osage grade. Lamps were lighted and little jots of rain dashed against the lenses as the stage struggled up the slick trail. Harry, always uneasy with anyone else driving, heard the heavily ironed wheels grind against flinty rocks while dripping branches constantly lashed the side curtains. Running slow, they changed teams and drivers at a lonely home station in a grove of dark trees, and had a supper of bread, tea, and cold fried venison for forty cents. Then the weary passengers trudged out to the coach numb with discouragement and fatigue.

The tall man, Brown, occupied a seat to himself in the front, facing the others. He lay down across the seat, his valise under his head, and slept. The hard jawed man at the other side of the girl slumped and tried to sleep. Harry could see the girl's head dropping forward every now and then. Finally she turned to him and murmured, 'Mr. Logan, a girl can hardly sleep on the shoulder of a man who doesn't even know her name. But if I don't sleep I'll die. So I'll tell you: It's Judith Russell. The bear on my left is my father-in-law. Please wake me up at San Francisco.'

With her head composed on his shoulder, she reached back and pulled her bonnet off. Harry tingled. Then there was a feeling of comfort in him; properly or not, he had made a friend. He had just been thinking that only the grave could house a loneliness like his.

In the morning they reached a little town high among some rugged mountains. The stage ran past brick fronts dark with rain. The air was heavy with breakfast smoke and mist, but the rain had stopped.

The girl smiled and stretched. The stage passed through a gate into a yard. A man with a beard which looked as though mice had been at it opened the door.

'Ladies and gentlemen, this is Fayetteville, Arkansas. This is a meal and change station. You'll have plenty of time to eat at Van Winkle's Hotel. When you come back, your luggage will have been transferred to the Troy coach yonder. What it lacks in comfort it makes up otherwise. The benches make down into a bed, and you can hardly tip one of them over.'

Arkansas! Harry roused, stepped out quickly and helped Judith down. He got a smile for thanks as she hurried off with the other passengers to find the hotel. Just then he heard a horse jog into the yard from an alley. He watched the rider dismount and relinquish his horse to a hostler. His knee-length boots were plastered with mud and his heavy short-coat was stained.

'What's the word?' the station agent asked quickly.

'The word is that thirty miles is a hell of a distance to ride, not to find out anything. I went as far as Parks'. Nothing doing. Not a whisper of that coach anywhere.'

'Any guerrillas about?' the agent asked quickly.

'Been some activity beyond Fort Smith, I gather. But nothing between here and Smith.'

'Well . . .' The agent scowled in thought. 'Well, I'll send 'em on, I reckon.' Then, seeing Harry watching, he smiled nervously and added, 'Nothing to get excited about. The eastbound didn't get through last night. No doubt you'll pass her somewhere, up to the bolsters in mud.'

Harry left the yard. Across from the station was a muddy, treeless little square where a small group of men were drilling with guns and broomsticks. The war, which had been a

56

politician's pastime until recently, was finally spreading like a stain beyond the Mississippi. Before the hotel, Harry saw the grey-eyed passenger, Brown, watching them with a smile of disdain.

'Look at them,' he said to Harry. 'When the command is right, half of them go left and the rest bear dead ahead.'

Smiling, Harry watched the drill sergeant try to salvage something from a right-flank order. 'You an army man?' he asked.

'No,' shrugged Brown, 'but I know my right hand from my left. And don't tell me it's different when you're carrying a rifle. Your right's your right whether you're toting a gun or a pitchfork.' He went into the hotel.

There was something cold and mean about him, Harry thought as he took a seat at the far end of the long table where the stage passengers were being served. Bowls of hominy and platters of tough steak were arranged along the table. Harry helped himself. He ate a few bites and began wondering whether Kelsey had eaten at this table too. He closed his eyes and seemed to feel her presence in the room, and the sickness of loss came back to him.

A heavy hand came down on his shoulder and a hearty voice said, 'They do say the grub ain't bad here, friend Logan. Reckon we'll survive it?'

The man jostled Harry as he swung his leg

57

over the bench and got settled. Harry did not move. He sat with his hands drawing warmth from his coffee mug. 'Don't risk the food on my account,' he said. 'I'll chance anything, you know. Sometimes I even make it pay off.'

Pete Canty chuckled. 'That was some rain, eh? You shoulda been out in it on a horse! I used up eight company nags getting here.'

'The rain seemed to let up after we left Missouri,' observed Harry. 'They say everything's different down here in Arkansas.'

'Is that right? Some things you can control better than the weather, though. For instance, I carry a letter from the president of the Missouri and Arkansas Rail Road that makes friends out of strangers sometimes.'

A little way down the table, Judith Russell was silently picking at her food while her father-in-law stared stiffly at Harry as he listened to the conversation.

Harry spooned damp brown sugar into his coffee. 'What've you got from the Attorney General?' he asked.

Canty chuckled. 'Attorney General!— Where do you pick up all those big words?'

'People teach me. I see somebody taught you something too.' He was looking at the bruise under Canty's left eye.

A mean memory rose to Canty's face. 'Yes, sir, somebody sure did. Somebody I never thought could teach me so much as which end of a shovel was dirty. But my God, he handed

58

me the dirty end, and I took it. But I'm going to give it back some day, Logan.'

Harry saw the bulge under his coat. 'Who are you working for now?' he asked him.

'I'm working for Canty—the meanest boss a man ever had. You might say I've been working for him all my life, and always will, because he won't fire me and I can't quit. I'd be afraid to go back to Missouri without that money, just for what he'd say to me. It's double eagles to horseshoes that I get it, too.'

Harry said, 'I wouldn't know about the money. All I'm after is a girl.' He stood up and signalled the proprietor. The Russells watched him. 'Will I be seeing you?' he asked Canty.

'All the way,' said Canty. 'I'll never get that job back unless I come back with the money: so you're the bloodhound I'll trail it with. Set a thief to catch one. After that—don't be surprised at anything.'

Harry left. He had ten minutes still, and he spent them on exercise, walking about the square. If there was nothing Canty could do about him, he realized, there was nothing he could do about Canty. Canty was the balanced rock above the trail; the priming-cap hungry for powder. Wherever Harry led, Canty would follow.

Across the square, passengers were trailing back to the depot. Harry walked back, leaning against a wind that was tearing holes in the clouds to find a sky the colour of skim milk.

The old coach had disappeared and the mud-wagon stood ready. Harry saw the coach tip slightly and knew passengers were already aboard. He heard a man speaking.

'Now do you see where flirting with stage tramps can lead you? A thief, by heaven!'

'He's no thief,' Judith Russell contradicted, with a yawn.

'Oh, you know all about him, do you?'

'As much as you do. The man was just speaking in parables, like the prophets. Why didn't he arrest Harry, if he's a thief?'

'I couldn't say, but I'll make it my business to find out. Perhaps with a little encouragement he'd have your friend jailed and sent back to Missouri!'

'Don't bother,' Judith advised. 'I'll find out from Harry what the trouble was. I'll have everything straightened out in no time.'

Passengers were coming into the yard. Harry heard Russell say, with a bite, 'As you straightened things out for my son?'

'Father,' sighed the girl, 'I *begged* Louis not to join up. But he would be riding off to war. And after all, isn't our cross the same one every relative carries when a man goes to war?'

'Yes, but you see some take it more courageously than others. Miss Judith, you may think that by marrying Louis you bought yourself a ticket to Happy Valley! Well, not if I can help it.'

Harry walked back to the street. He was

60

sorry he had heard it, because it would be hard to be natural with either of them now; but that was an annoyance, not a worry. And the worry in him carried him inside to talk to the station keeper. He found him whirling the wheel of a letter press down on an onion-skin volume. Harry waited until he looked up.

'Say, I just heard about those train robbers going through here last week,' he said. 'Pretty tough customers, eh? Did you get a look at them?'

The agent paused. 'Now, that's the queer thing about it. The man was so ordinary he didn't even make a dent. But the girl I recollect. She was dressed well enough, but mighty light in case they hit cold weather. And very pretty—tall and fairish. I wouldn't have guessed she was a bad one, but there it is on my waybill: *Mr. and Mrs. Reuben Geary.* Wrong name—right people.'

He suddenly glanced up at the clock. 'Jupiter!' He pulled a mail-sack from beneath the counter, padlocked it, and just then the conductor came in from the yard to pick it up.

## CHAPTER EIGHT

At Brodie's Station that night they lowered the hard seat backs to form a bed and drew lots to select the three who would sleep first. The losers rode outside or cramped together on a seat which had not been let down. Harry was one of the first to sleep. Later that night he listened to Russell grumbling about the Oxbow service, and saw him finally sit up in the cold, jarring darkness to raise a leather curtain an inch and stare out. Judith was sleeping as soundly as a cat. Even Canty, after his all-night, rain-soaked ride, seemed to sleep. Russell searched his coat and found a broken cigar. He ignited a wax match from a little block of them. Raising it, he discovered Harry watching drowsily from his corner. In the yellow light, Russell's mouth was down-curving and harsh. He had the eyes and loose jowls of an old bulldog, but under the flabby skin were jaws like a trap. A wheel dropped into a hole, and the flame was thrust almost into his eye. Russell swore.

'You can take this line and John Butterfield and dump them in the Mississippi,' he snapped.

'Well, let's not dump them till we reach' Frisco,' Harry suggested.

Russell got the cigar going and dropped the wicklike match out the window. 'Do you know what we'd haul in wagons like this in New York State? Hogs! Freight and hogs! To put human beings on planks for three weeks and expect them to survive it . . .'

There was a dry chuckling of sand-boxes and tarred axles. Harry was annoyed. 'The point is, this isn't New York,' he argued. 'Out here it's mud-wagons or nothing.'

Russell's eyes moved over Harry's plain brown suit. 'You wouldn't be Butterfield himself, now?'

'I had three coaches, sixteen head of stock, and forty miles of road out of Burnsville,' Harry told him.

Russell shrugged. 'I had an interest in a line once myself. So I'm not guessing when I say you can't beat passengers to death, feed them slops, and keep their trade.'

Harry smiled. 'But John Butterfield's got the mail contracts. If somebody thinks he can parallel his line without help from Uncle Sam, let him tackle it.'

'You wouldn't be forgetting the central route?' Russell challenged. 'It's shorter, and there's feed and water all year. *Politics* drove the line south—not common sense. A Secesh president and postmaster-general. And now, with the war on, Congress still lets a bungler like Butterfield pack the mail.'

Suddenly Harry had the impression that Russell, for some reason, had done a lot of talking and thinking about the transcontinental stage routes. He asked Russell, 'If you don't like the southern route, why not let Butterfield move the line north? He's the man with the stock and the experience.'

Russell did not reply. Puffing on the cigar,

he settled on one elbow and muttered, 'It must be almost time for me to relinquish this featherbed to some other lucky passenger.'

Through the night the stage teetered along steep ravines and climbed masses of broken rock. In the darkness the lamps glowed like cat's eyes, and the harsh cries of the driver came back like cries for help. In the dawn the coach crossed a pass, and before it lay a long sweep of forest. Far in the distance there was the flash of the reddened water of some great river.

Later in the morning they ferried the Arkansas and rolled on to Fort Smith where three thousand people had built a miracle city in the wilderness. Hotels, saloons and churches mingled, and cavalrymen from the big fort up on the bluff rode the streets. Harry felt the bounding pulse of a town elated with success. This was the sentry-box of civilization—the largest community between Independence and Los Angeles; the last place where you could count on American food, women, or supplies. And it came to him with a jolt that Lute Harper might have thought the same thing— might have decided to leave the stage at Fort Smith, lay in supplies, and cut south-east to Little Rock or Memphis. When the coach stopped at the mail agency, Harry brushed past Pete Canty and went into the waiting room. A big man wearing paper sleeve-protectors stood behind the counter.

'Do you know anything about a couple named Greary?' Harry asked. 'They went through here on the last westbound.'

The agent scrutinized him. He laid a pencil over his ear, turned, and began searching through a grille of pigeonholes. 'Is your name Logan?'

Harry felt his mouth drying. 'Yes.' Now he heard the war-weary veterans of the mountain-crossing shuffling into the room. Glancing around, he saw Canty approaching, grim and unshaven. The lady passengers were going through a door on one side of the room and the men on the other. The conductor dropped the mail-sacks behind the counter. Canty moved in beside Harry. Harry pressed his arm against the gun beneath his coat to reassure himself that it was there.

From one of the pigeonholes the agent drew a letter. For a long time he stood scowling at it, as though his vision had penetrated the envelope and he was reading what was inside. Harry had a sick feeling of suspense.

'Logan, eh?' muttered the agent. 'I reckon this is yours, then.' He offered it grumpily, as though it were his right to know what was in it.

Harry held the letter in both hands; he wanted to handle it as carefully as a butterfly, as firmly as a gold-piece. He started to tear it open, but stopped and glanced at Canty.

'Go ahead,' Canty encouraged. 'Not that it'll be much help to you—being as you can't read it anyway.'

'It'll keep,' Harry said. 'Where do we eat in this town?' he asked the agent.

'City Hotel. Yonder—across the street.'

As Harry was leaving, Judith came from the ladies' room carrying her bonnet. 'Did you find where to eat?' she asked him. 'I'm starved. I'm not going to wait for father.'

*     *     *

Within the big dining-room there were wonderful steamy odours of frying meat, coffee, and yeast bread. They took seats at a small table. Harry glanced at her gown, dove-grey and closely fitted, with a row of tiny buttons down the front and a prim white collar. It looked neat and expensive. He glanced up and she was smiling at his attention.

'Yes, it did cost quite a lot—if that's what you were thinking. But then there's a lot to spend. And I didn't steal it, eith—' She gasped. 'Oh, I shouldn't have said that!' She stared at him.

Harry looked at the letter by his plate. He didn't think it was a slip, but he was glad she had said it, because he could clarify things now. Probably that was what she wanted. He said, 'Canty wasn't talking in parables. He meant it about setting a thief to catch a thief. Sure—I did some listening, too,' he smiled.

'Accidentally. Thanks for standing up for me. Will you do something else?'

The long-lashed eyes studied him. Her face was quick, a little thin, much more than emptily pretty. She might act impetuously, but not until she had made up her mind to. 'Probably,' she said.

Harry picked up the letter. 'Someone left this for me at the station. I can't read very well, and it looks like she wrote it while the stage was moving. But I've got to know what it says before we pull out again. Because I might have to get off here.'

Judith glanced at the sheet, turned it over, and said, 'Your friend Canty is at the table behind you. Lean close so I can whisper. *Harry, Dear:*' she read softly. '*I am writing this in the stage at night. Lute is asleep. I am going as far as El Paso with him, because if I did get away sooner Canty might catch up with me before you do. I will wait for you there.*

'*I pray that you are all right.*

'*Lute forced me to sign the bills—all of them. And then I was afraid to go back. Oh, Harry, what*—It isn't signed,' Judith said disappointedly.

Harry leaned on his forearms, frowning at his meshed fingers. 'Her name is Kelsey Harper. Her brothers pulled a train robbery in Missouri and they managed to drag her into the mess too. Lute Harper killed a railroad guard and took off. Canty's after him. At least

I know she got this far,' he said. He didn't tell her about Canty's plans for him.

'Is Canty after the girl too?'

'Yes, now that he knows she signed the banknotes. He's—' He shook his head. 'He's like a wolf. Staying near my campfire, waiting for me to fall asleep.'

'Are you going to stop him before we reach El Paso?'

Harry looked at her. She seemed concerned, not inquisitive. 'What do you think?'

'I think it would serve him right if you did— We'd better eat,' she added. She ate a few bites but never stopped frowning. 'There are three kinds of people, Harry: Good ones, like my father-in-law. Bad ones, like us. And the rotten ones who hunt the bad ones so people won't notice how rotten they are.'

'What's bad about you?'

'Women who marry for money are the worst kind of women there are,' Judith explained. 'Because they give away the secret—that a woman is nobody unless she can catch a man with money.'

Harry laughed. 'You couldn't help it if the man you married had money.'

'Yes, I could. I saw to it that I didn't marry anyone who didn't have money.' Her smile was clear and frank. 'And that took some doing. The trick is to make him want you, and think he's going to get you. But then he finds he isn't

68

going to get you anywhere but in church, even if you are just a sort of a dancer who sings a little. Or a sort of singer who dances a little.'

Harry was embarrassed. He was unused to hearing women talk so plainly. He remembered what Kelsey had told him about getting his start before they married. It was the same speech, only it sounded different when Kelsey said it. Kelsey didn't say, *You won't do.* She said: *We'll have to wait.*

'We might as well go back,' Judith said. 'We aren't eating anyway.'

As they passed Canty's table, Canty leaned back and caught Harry's coat. 'What do you hear from the gang?' he said, grinning.

'They're heading for Wyoming to trap muskrat,' Harry told him.

'That puts us in practically the same business,' said Canty.

\*        \*        \*

'We'll be in the Choctaw Nation tonight,' Judith said, in the street. 'Maybe you could lose him there.'

Harry had been thinking the same thing. She took his arm as they walked across the ruts of the street. 'You must think I'm insane to come on a trip like this,' she said.

'You need a good reason,' Harry admitted.

'I've got one: Father Russell had to go to California on business. He has a partner in San

Francisco he doesn't trust. He brought me along because he was afraid I'd spend all Louis's money if I were left alone. But,' she smiled, 'I brought enough along to tide me over. And I sent some more by clipper to San Francisco in case I decide to stay.'

'Sounds like everything's taken care of,' said Harry.

'Everything except Mr. Canty,' said Judith. 'If I can help you there, I will.'

'I'll manage,' Harry said. *Maybe I'm getting suspicious,* he thought. Because he was beginning to wonder about her concern for him. Just before they boarded the stage he saw Canty speaking to her. He wished keenly that he had not had to trust her so far. But after she flashed a smile across the room at him, he was almost ashamed of suspecting her. She was quite a girl. Louis probably hadn't had a prayer.


# CHAPTER NINE

On Sunday they ferried the Red River and were in Texas. The Choctaw Nation was behind now; but Pete Canty was still on the passenger list, always seeming to be one foot behind Harry, a fighter who never let himself be coaxed out of position. One of these mornings they would roll into some station and find that Kelsey's stage had been held back because of guerrilla activity or Indian trouble; and Canty would strike so fast it would be over before Harry woke up. So long as Canty needed him, Harry was safe. Once Canty cut sign on his quarry, Harry was under the gun. *I've got to ditch him*, he realized desperately. He couldn't help Kelsey or himself with Canty on his back. Judith had said she would help, if she could. How could she help? Travelling like this, how could he make any plans at all? Banging along from station to station—*Ten minutes, folks! Forty minutes for dinner, folks! Hurry up, folks! Ladies will find wild flowers to the right of the road; gents will enjoy the scenery to the left*—they were like prisoners in custody of the driver and conductor.

Behind six horses, leaving the Nations far behind, the stage went swerving and lunging south-west through the Cross Timbers, over gullied roads where dust sifted like face powder through the coach, roughening the skin and putting the teeth on edge. Tortured-looking oaks and blackjack grew on the rolling hills. Mules replaced the stage horses one morning and there was a falling-off in the quality of meals. Jerky, mesquite beans and hoe-cake with alkali water was the menu after that. Russell fumed like a wet fire. Canty grew more hard-bitten. The lean-faced man named Brown, who never spoke to anyone when he could answer with a shrug, became oddly cheerful. At Gunnison's Station one night he asked for coffee.

'Coffee!' laughed Eli Gunnison, wiping dirty hands on his trousers. 'What's that—some nasty habit you picked up in the city?' He was a sour-faced man with a large, naked-looking nose, large ears, and a mouth firmly enclosed between two deep creases.

As they were finishing their meal, he broke the news. 'You'll sleep without wheels under you tonight, folks. This stage won't leave until five a.m.'

'What's the idea?' asked Canty.

'Guerrillas. They ain't afraid of the dark like Injuns. They raided a ranch near here today and took all the stock and vittles.'

'Then why don't we have a military escort?' demanded Russell.

'That's a good question. You take it up with Butterfield. You might ask him too how this here westbound is going to get through Arizona when the eastbounds have all been stopped.'

'How do you know they've been stopped?' Harry asked.

'A little express rider told me. He passed through an hour ago. The word is that the Injuns have finally broke the mail road like a rotten fish line. No coaches have come through from Arizona for six days. And none can get farther than El Paso.'

Knives and forks were quietly laid down. 'Now don't get gooseflesh over it,' advised the tender. 'There's military forts out there, and they'll soon put a ring in the big chiefs' noses and get the mail rolling again. Some of you men want to help me carry in straw for the ladies' beds? Gents will sleep in the barn.'

'Is there a saddle-horse I can rent?' a man asked.

Harry glanced down the table. It was Brown, sitting erect and looking tartly at Gunnison. 'What's the hurry?' the agent asked.

Brown stood up, wiping his mouth on a bandanna. 'My ticket's only for Fort Belknap, anyhow. I'll cut across country and catch a ride with a freight-string for Galveston.'

'Suit yourself. I've a green-broke filly you can have for twenty dollars, if you can handle her. What ailed you to take the stage, if you was going to Galveston? You could've took a steamboat to N'Yorlins and a steamship from there.'

'There was a blockade above Memphis,' said Brown. He went outside and came back with his small travelling case. Gunnison issued a refund on his ticket. Brown passed a cool and superior smile over the others who were making beds. 'Well, friends, I wish you luck. If you're ever in Galveston, take a boat to my sugar-mill up the Brazos.'

Twenty minutes later they heard him profanely bringing the filly into line, and shortly after he was gone into the post-oak and blackjack thickets.

Harry and the other men carried in the not-too-clean straw and made a long pallet the length of one wall. Atop this, canvases were spread as ticking. As Harry left, Judith called to him; she was sitting on a bench near the fireplace, looking perplexedly at a little pearl-handled pocket pistol.

'I suppose I should load this, shouldn't I?' she said. 'But I can't remember how the man in the store said to load it. I bought it in the East.'

'I hope you've got powder and ball too,' said Harry.

She produced them from her large petit-point bag. Harry loaded the five chambers and set the hammer carefully on safety. 'That's no toy,' he warned. 'It's a good thing for a young woman to carry, but a bad one to drop.'

'Better than smelling salts, I've heard,' Judith said.

The conductor came in from the yard and Harry saw him poking about the room. Then he stopped near the fire and chewed on his sandy moustache a moment. 'Folks,' he called suddenly. The room was silent, and his tight-skinned red face looked shiny in the firelight. 'Did any of you carry the mail pouch away from the stage?'

Naturally no one had. The conductor looked at Gunnison, and the driver walked in and looked at them both. 'All right, you men,' rapped the conductor, 'get your side arms, any that's packing them. That son-of-a—that what's-his-name—Brown—stole the mail pouch when he left!'

Gunnison ran out to rustle up horses. The yard was full of men saddling. Harry drew a blanket and surcingle. He saw Pete Canty mounted on a high-horn saddle, waiting calmly. Looking at him, Harry felt a stroke of excitement. The ladies were watching from the open door and the windows. Judith was standing just outside the door. Glinting in her hand was the little pistol Harry had loaded for her. She spoke as he prepared to mount.

'You wouldn't need my gun, too, would you? You're welcome to it.'

'If I can't drop him with six of my own shots, I'm dead already,' Harry said.

Judith lowered her voice, smiling in her special, secret way. 'If you don't get Brown, maybe you'll get something just as good . . .'

'I'm hoping I will,' Harry muttered.

He led his horse out to mount, feigned trouble in mounting with stirrup, and led it to a stone corral wall. A confusion of lead-ropes and harness were dragged across the wall. As he mounted, he caught up a good cotton rope and folded it across his horse's withers.

'Let's go!' shouted Wiley, the conductor.

It was a crisp, quiet night with no moon yet. Wiley used a dark-lamp now and then to

75

investigate hoof-tracks. There had been little recent traffic on the road, and no running traffic except Brown. Two miles west of the station he had turned south into the blackjack thickets. After that it was mean going. There was a lot of small deadfall which caused the horses to stumble, and the trees were big enough to make seeing anything difficult. They lost the trail at last and were slow in picking it up again.

'Split up!' barked Wiley. 'Anybody cuts his sign, fire two fast shots. Keep whistlin' till we find you.'

Some of the men were slow at separating. By nature, most men were shoulder-to-shoulder posse men. But Harry quirted his pony and it broke south through the stirrup-high brush, finding little animal trails Harry could scarcely see. He rode this way for a few minutes, and then hurriedly pulled off left and cut back towards the mail road on a parallel line. He jumped down and tied the horse to a hackberry and, standing quietly, listened a moment. Far off he heard horses plunging around in the brush. But one of them was closer and heading his way: Canty was sticking to him like a shrewish wife.

Harry had tied the pony only a hundred feet from the trail he had been on before he reversed his direction. Now, hurrying towards it, he looked for a lightning blasted hackberry he had noticed as he rode down. Suddenly he saw it: An off-balance affair with one grey, arthritic arm extending like a hay beam above the ground. Harry stood under the tree and measured. The limb was too high to catch. There were no helpful lower branches, and he heard the horseman crowding along faster, as though anxious to palaver with Harry out here away from everyone else.

And it hit Harry like a wet sack: He had thought he was hunting Canty, but Canty was hunting him! The dectective didn't need him any more. He knew Lute and Kelsey were going no farther than El Paso, he could be sure of finding them there. So he was coming out here to settle things with Harry Logan, his personal angel of bad luck.

Harry flipped the end of the rope he had brought over the limb, close to the trunk of the tree. He kept flipping it until the end wiggled down to where he could catch it. Then, holding both ends of the rope doubled together, he climbed until he could catch the limb. Once he was crouched upon it, huddled against the trunk of the tree, he felt terribly vulnerable, for there was little to hide him.

A minute or two after he got settled, he heard the rider moving in the brush a few rods north of him. The trail he had taken was fairly plain here, an old deer trail. He heard the horse sidle, and then a man grunted harshly, 'Hah!' as he curbed it. Then he was coming on again. First Harry saw the black shape of the rider above the post-oak, leaning sideways to look for tracks as he rode along. Then the horse broke into the open twenty feet away, tossing its head as it came along. The horse sniffed Harry and shied. But Canty muttered a curse and banged it over the head with his hat; evidently it was a shying animal and he was tired of its false leads. Now it was passing beneath the hackberry. Harry poised himself and dropped.

Canty was riding with his pistol in his hand. As Harry fell on him the horse went squealing and buck-jumping aside; but Harry had Canty by his big shoulders and they fell on the ground. With the horse tearing off through the thickets they were alone, Harry slugging desperately at Canty's head as the big, tobacco-smelling man under him fought back. Canty fought like a man scared but wild, lunging and reaching back to catch hold of any part of Harry's clothing to pull him off. Harry held his fist cocked, and smashed at Canty's jaw as he turned his head to try to see his attacker. Clean and hard, his knuckles jarred Canty's chin. Canty loosened, and Harry hit him again. Canty still was not quite out, but he wasn't fighting any more. Harry pulled his arms behind him, made a good, solid horseman's lashing about his wrists, another about his ankles, and tied wrists and ankles together. With Canty beginning to stir, he used Canty's own handkerchief to gag him. He made sure the knots were hard, snatched up his hat from the ground and ran back to his horse.

Somewhere a man fired two shots and commenced whistling shrilly. Harry groped through the brush towards the sound. He didn't think Canty had even seen him during the fight. He rode on until he heard a few men talking, joining them where Wiley's little dark-lantern was flicking about the ground like a firefly.

'What's up?' Harry asked.

'Don't know,' grunted the conductor. 'Could be Brown's tracks, could be one of them guerrillas Gunnison was talking about.'

They followed the trail with less and less zest, until finally someone said, 'This is no damn use, boys. What we're gonna get is shot, all of us. Let's get back. What's a mail pouch more or less?'

'My job, that's all,' mourned Wiley.

No one noticed Canty's absence until they were unsaddling in the yard. But no one wanted to go back and look for him. 'Likely he'll find the road eventually and come wandering in to break our rest,' said one man.

\*     \*     \*

It was about four in the morning, with a watery grey in the east. The stage men were already stirring, preparing for the early start, when a

79

man shambled into the barn. Harry was awake. Lying there, staring up at the dark ceiling, he heard the conductor mutter, 'What the hell happened to you?'

'Good question,' growled Canty's voice.

'You look like you'd tangled with a cross-bred catamount.'

'I don't know what I tangled with. It might have been Brown. On the other hand it might have been a tree-climbing varmint of some kind. I'd appreciate it if somebody would untie my wrists. My teeth got a little sore working on the knots around my ankles.' After Wiley obliged him, Canty said, 'Now, I'm going to lay down here and get some rest while you get ready to travel. I'll kill the man who wakes me up before stage time, and I'll catch up and kill you if you leave me.'

Wiley chuckled nervously.

Canty, settling himself on the straw, asked, 'I hope you didn't lose any sleep fretting over me being lost?'

'We searched quite a spell,' lied the conductor, 'but finding anything in that brush is like stalking a flea in your underwear.'

At five-thirty the stage horn blew. Canty came trotting from the barn, beating straw from his coat, and took his place. He and Harry faced each other stolidly across the coach. At last Harry said, 'Saved you a seat, Canty.'

Canty said, 'Thanks very much. I'm saving

you something too.'

All morning the mail coach rocked along through arroyos and scraped through dry thickets.

The growth was becoming more dry and worthless; the ground was as hard and scaly as hoof-parings. About nine o'clock, as the stage crossed a wide, lonely plateau, there was a popping sound from ahead like a cork being drawn; then several more reports which were suddenly louder, and abruptly the coach faltered. There was some shouting. Canty crawled over a woman to put his head out the window. He drew back and gazed at the others with a strange, tight-lipped expression.

'If any of you men are carrying guns,' he said, 'I wouldn't advise going for them. There's a couple of dozen fellows up yonder with rifles.'

The woman at Canty's side began screaming. He matter-of-factly slapped her mouth and she stopped. 'We'll be murdered,' she wailed.

'No, we won't,' Canty said. 'I expect they're guerrillas. Most likely all they want is money or weapons.'

Harry thought of the canvas belt about his waist, and numbly felt for it under his shirt. Twelve hundred dollars in gold . . . In all his life he might never save that much again. He had sold his boyhood for it, his chance to be educated above anything more than a ploughhorse.

'Give it to me—quickly!' whispered Judith. 'They won't go through my clothes for it.' He gazed blankly at her. 'Isn't it a money belt?' she asked.

Harry pulled his shirt open, groped for the buckle and unfastened it. With Canty and Russell watching, he pulled out the dully clinking belt with its heavy pockets. Judith pulled up her bodice and wrapped it about her waist. Tucked up under the waistband of her skirt was the little pistol Harry had loaded for her.

'*Judith!*' snapped her father-in-law.

Judith said mildly, 'Do hush up.' There was a foot of belt left over, which she tucked down inside her skirt.

An instant later, as Harry glanced out, he saw a line of horsemen come loping past and pull up quickly. The coach was surrounded. Judith sat close to Harry, beginning to tremble as she saw their rifles and revolvers. Harry reached to squeeze her hand, but found her thigh. Later he remembered how, though her leg was slender, it felt soft.

In the road a man was shouting, 'Keep your heads and nobody will get hurt. Driver, stay up there and hold your horses. Conductor, throw down the express box. You passengers—light down, now, with your hands up.'

Judith stared at Harry. 'Why, that—that sounds like Mr. Brown!'

The door was yanked open. They looked out at a thin, hard man in a grey hickory-cloth shirt and dark pants who held a revolver in his hand. 'Out,' he said.

They lined up in the road. Canty, who had been hoping for this moment, got out last and in dismounting he bumped into Harry, who lurched forward: the man with the revolver quickly levelled it at Harry's stomach. Harry felt something being slipped into his coat pocket. He looked around at the railroad man. But Canty was now meekly taking his place in line with his hands raised.

A horseman paced along the line, sternly looking them over. It was Brown. Enormously aware of his position, he gazed down on the passengers. He wore a loose black coat with big pockets, and fine ox-blood riding boots coming above his knees. On the side of his head rested a shallow, wide-brimmed black hat curled on the edges like a meat platter. He was mounted on a deep-chested grey with a blanket roll behind the saddle. Suddenly he smiled.

'Well, friends, we meet again. I regret disturbing you, but you needn't be frightened. No one will be harmed. There is something religious about any great cause, and it seems appropriate that we should be taking up a collection for Jefferson Davis.

'Miss Russell,' said Brown chivalrously, 'you are uncommonly pretty even when disturbed.

You may lower your hands. You other ladies also.'

Judith brought her hands down and slipped halfway behind Harry.

'Captain Matthew Thomas is my real name,' said ex-passenger Brown. 'Affiliated, you might say, with the Eleventh Texas. I regret visiting this inconvenience on you but as you know it costs money to fight a war. If any of you is carrying a money belt, I'll ask you to disengage it and drop it on the road.'

Russell cleared his throat. 'The company doesn't permit large amounts of money to be carried.'

'Oh, I know. But I can't believe a man wearing such fine clothes as you would be carrying less than several hundred dollars. Corporal Sams, will you pass the hat? Take any weapons you find while you're at it.'

A big, keen, rather violent-looking man with over-full moustaches dismounted. He pushed his Dragoon pistol into a holster and started down the line with a linen sack opened for contributions. Up forward there was a shot and Harry pushed Judith back against the coach. Then he saw that one of the guerrillas had shot the lock from the express box. Corporal Sams's pale, sharp eyes were digging at Harry's face, now. He took Harry's revolver from its shoulder holster and then held the sack out to him.

Harry pulled a handful of gold and silver

84

from his pocket. The corporal sorted the coins as Harry held them on his palm. 'Forty-two-fifty? That wouldn't have left you much of a stake when you reached California, friend. Where's the rest?'

'That's all there is. I was going to have to land some work. I've got a hundred and fifty dollars sunk in my ticket.'

The corporal glanced around. 'How about it, Captain?'

'Search his pockets.'

While the corporal went through Harry's pockets, Captain Thomas shifted in the saddle. 'I expect you're curious as to how I happened to be travelling with you. Well, it was a little purchasing expedition. To my dismay I found that in the East nothing but gold is classed as money. You may also wonder why I bothered taking the mail pouch when I planned meeting you all here anyway. Well, there was always the chance you might delay; and my superiors can't wait for the kind of information the mail often carries—what do you have there, Corporal Sams?'

The corporal was inspecting an envelope he had taken from Harry's coat. Harry studied it too. It was unfamiliar. As the guerrilla passed it up to Captain Thomas, Harry turned his head to look at Canty. Canty continued to gaze across the road at the dry post-oak thickets.

After a glance at the contents of the envelope, the captain regarded Harry severely.

'Fall out over yonder,' he said. 'Stand by that last trooper.'

Harry clenched his fists. 'I don't know what's in that, but I'll tell you who put it there—Canty!'

Thomas wearily smiled at the others. 'I daresay I'll be hearing a great deal of this before the war is over,' he said. 'Fall out.'

'Good luck,' murmured Canty as Harry passed him.

When the corporal had finished taking up the collection, he brought the heavy sack to Thomas. Hefting it with one hand, the captain smiled. 'Now will you all get back inside? You see, it wasn't so bad. No—stay where you are,' he told Harry sharply.

As the others mounted the coach, Judith advanced towards the captain. 'Why are you keeping him? Isn't he coming with us?'

'No, ma'am. I want to ask him some questions about this letter he's carrying.'

'But, he—he can't read. It can't be his.'

'Someone he was planning to contact can read. Step inside, Miss Russell.'

Biting her lip, Judith looked helplessly at Harry. 'Harry—' she said uncertainly.

'Don't worry,' Harry said. He remembered his money belt, which did not seem very important at the moment. But he suddenly remembered something else. 'If you kissed me good-bye,' he smiled, 'I'd feel better about it, though. All right with you, Captain?'

Thomas shrugged. 'If you can wheedle one out of the young lady.'

Judith hurried up the road to Harry and put her arms around him. He held her close, pressing his face against her hair. 'Quick—put your gun in my pocket,' he whispered.

Judith leaned back, gazing earnestly into his face. 'Oh, Harry . . .You will take care?' she pleaded. Her hand fumbled at her dress. A moment later she buried her face against his coat, sobbing, and Harry felt a small, wonderful weight drop into his coat pocket.

'All right, all right,' barked Thomas angrily. 'I didn't say you could marry the girl. Inside, please, Miss Russell.' His thin face had reddened. The mean and wire-tight nature Harry had seen in him before was rising.

Judith was led to the stagecoach, helped inside, and the door was slammed. As the horses plunged forward, Harry felt the hugeness of the plains picking him up like a straw in a cyclone. *Four days by stage to El Paso . . . how many days on foot?*

The dust drifted off, and the harness jingled as the guerrillas assembled in the road. 'Tie his hands behind him,' said Captain Thomas. 'I daresay there's a trick or two left in him.'

# CHAPTER TEN

A mile south of the road the guerrillas had a camp in a gully. Mesquite and ragged little oaks grew thickly along the stratified limestone banks. Flash-floods had undercut the ledges, and beneath the overhang supplies were stored. There were a few barrels half sheltered by a canvas, and a portable forge in the back of a wagon. The smoke of cook fires had blackened the limestone at two or three points. While the rebels tended their horses, Captain Thomas sat on a box reading the paper he had taken from Harry. Harry had been untied, and sat on the sand with a man guarding him. Thomas rose and paced up and down for a moment.

'Who is A. G. McNary?' he asked Harry suddenly.

'I don't know.'

*'Who is McNary?'* shouted the captain.

Harry shook his head. 'I never heard of him.'

'Then how do you happen to be carrying a letter addressed to him?'

'I told you, Canty put it in my pocket.'

Thomas put his fists on his hips, the paper crumpled in one hand. 'Keep on lying to me,' he said, 'and you'll hang with a lie in your mouth. Answer my questions and I may let you go.'

Suddenly Harry understood why he had not hanged him already. Whatever Canty had written, it apparently hinted at something Thomas was determined to learn. 'Captain,' he said, 'I can't tell you any more than's in that letter.'

'Excuse me, Captain,' said the corporal. 'Maybe if the rest of us heard what's in it we might think of some questions to ask him.'

'It's for sure if *I* can't—' began the officer, 'Well, no harm in reading it to you. *Mr. A. G. McNary, Franklin, Texas: This will identify Mr. Harry Logan. Mr. Logan will tell you how funds may be moved to St. Louis in perfect safety. I can personally vouch for his honesty. Signed: F. Ashmore.*'

Thomas looked up at Harry and waited.

'I'll tell you all I know,' Harry said. 'Canty's a railroad detective. He's after some train robbers that went out on the stage ahead of ours. One of them was a girl who had nothing to do with it, and I'm trying to reach her before he does. I think he wrote that letter as soon as he knew we were in dangerous country and that the girl was in El Paso. He wanted me to get caught with it so I'd be held back, or killed.'

'Build a fire,' said Thomas to Corporal Sams.

Sams rubbed his squarish chin. 'What for, sir?' he asked uneasily.

'Damn you, Corporal, I said *build a fire.*'

Sams went to lay a fire under the ledge, while Thomas's suspicious eyes followed him. 'Now.' He turned to Harry. 'It's always seemed to me that the role of pain in warfare has been seriously maligned. Why is it any worse for a military officer to use pain to extract information from a prisoner than it is for a dentist to inflict it in extracting a tooth?'

'You'll get more teeth out of me than you will information,' Harry said.

'That's a risk I'm willing to take.'

The captain walked to a crate with its lid flung back and began groping through it. The young fellow who was guarding Harry glanced at Corporal Sams. Thomas spoke without looking around. 'Did you search him?'

'Yes, sir,' said Sams, with a wink at Harry's guard. 'That's where I found the letter.'

Thomas whirled with his teeth showing. 'I can break you to trooper in a hell of a hurry, Sergeant. This isn't a minstrel show, it's a—I meant did you *finish* searching him?'

Sams looked tired and disillusioned.

'Yes, sir. I looked for weapons before I started through his pockets. Took a good Colt off him.'

'All right.' Thomas continued gazing angrily at him. 'Some of you men who've had a little army service may think you can snicker at an officer who's only been to military school. Do you think so, Sams?'

90

'No, sir.'

'That's good. Now, you make the fires and tend the horses, and I'll run the troop! Clear?'

Sams said slowly, 'Yes, Captain. I understand.'

Harry rolled over on his side and watched the corporal add small mesquite branches to his kindling. Harry's hand rested on his hip; beneath it lay the gun Judith had dropped in his pocket. He watched the captain carry a rasp file to the fire. After laying it in the flames, he returned to squat beside Harry. His face was waxy with excitement. 'Do you remember anything about McNary, now? When and where he plans to take his money?'

'No.'

'Do you know how much gold he's trying to move north?'

'There is no such man,' said Harry.

'Well, so be it,' said Thomas, rising quickly. He returned to the fire to coddle the iron in the flames. Once he tried it against a piece of wood. Smoke curled and left a pattern of tiny triangles. Again he heated the file. Very thoroughly Harry was mapping the camp in his mind. On this side of the bank, working upstream, there were some bed rolls, himself and his guard, some crates, the fire, a pile of sacked goods under a tarred canvas. Across the stream bed, a line of horses were being tended. There were canvas buckets of water and a wooden barrel of grain. A man was rubbing the legs of the captain's grey with a gunny sack. Most of the horses had not been saddled; Harry liked that. Cinches had been loosened and a few horses had been unbridled and tied to the picket line.

Captain Thomas said tensely, 'Ready when you are, Corporal.'

As Corporal Sams walked towards him, Harry got to his feet. His hand dropped into the coat pocket. He found a side-hammer on the pistol and drew it back. Sams spoke to the man who had been guarding Harry. 'Catch his right arm, Lon.'

Harry backed away. The guerrillas followed him carefully. The captain approached with the smoking iron. The man on Harry's right feinted in at him, but drew back with a hiss of breath through his teeth. 'He's got something—what's in your pocket?' he shouted at Harry.

Harry drew the revolver and pointed it at Captain Thomas. 'It's small,' he said, 'but they say a rattle-snake doesn't have to be very big to kill a man.'

'Well, Corporal?' the captain said. 'I thought you searched him?'

'He did,' said Harry. 'The girl gave it to me when she kissed me good-bye. You by the grey horse—tighten the firth and lead it over here. Everybody else lie down.'

'I'll have you flogged if you do,' shouted

Thomas at the horse handler.

'I'll kill you if he doesn't,' said Harry. Several men were lying on the sand, but the others lagged. 'You've got five seconds to lie down,' Harry told them. 'Then I'll shoot the captain. You'll be next.'

With a sigh, Corporal Sams dropped to his knees. In a moment only Harry, Captain Thomas and the man bringing the horse were standing. Harry took the reins and the guerrilla trooper backed off and lay down on his belly.

'Captain, I meant you too,' Harry said.

'I think you'd better make me.' Thomas's thin, swarthy features were wild.

Harry pulled the reins over the horse's head and toed into the stirrup. Before putting his full weight on it, he tested the firth. It held, and he swung up. The captain backed a few feet, still holding the smoking file. Harry tugged at the reins and the horse backed. Glancing aside, he measured: twenty-five yards to the first bend downstream. He heard a man grunt with exertion. The file hit him on the side of the head and he smelled burned hair. As the horse tried to rear, Harry took him in hand sharply, staring grimly down at Captain Thomas who had started to pull his long-barrelled revolver.

'*No,*' Harry warned.

Thomas drew the gun. Harry squeezed the trigger of the little pistol. The roar was enormous and the pistol nearly jumped from his hand. The horse reared again. With the pistol butt, Harry tapped it between the ears and it dropped to its feet. The captain was raising the big Colt in both hands, though the side of his jaw had been torn away by Harry's bullet. Harry fired again. Captain Thomas fell forward. Harry wheeled the horse and loped down the stream bed. As he reached the turn he saw dust fly from the bank and heard the crash of a gun. More shots shook the narrow gully. He rode hard until he saw an opportunity to climb out of the arroyo.

Then he struck off west through the mesquite.

*     *     *

The grey was long-legged and powerful. It carried Harry easily through the tangles of small, dry trees. A half mile behind, he could see dust rising in a fan as the searchers spread out. Once he pulled in and listened. A few shots popped. Signals, he decided, or else they were firing at each other in the brush.

He came quite suddenly upon the mail road, a thread winding through the dry jungle of mesquite. Turning west, he let the horse out. A few minutes later when he reined in to rest it, he could hear nothing but the crisp rustling of birds in the brush. With the sun low and in his eyes, he jogged down the road.

Four miles west he came to a fortress-like station on the east bank of a dry creek. The walls were high and the brush had been cleared for several hundred feet around. A barred gate seemed to be the only entrance. Wheel-tracks rolled up to the gate; a second set emerged from the station and turned west. So the stage had come and gone. As he sat gazing towards the sun Harry heard bolts thudding back and the gate opened.

A deep-chested, hearty old man with a white beard and military moustache came out to motion him in. 'Get inside! I judge you're the man we were setting out to find, eh?'

Harry rode in. 'How long ago did the stage leave?' he asked.

'Nearly two hours ago, son. You'll never catch that one. They told us about you and kept going.'

Harry glanced about the large, corral like enclosure where mules, wagons and a well shared the space. The walls of this rectangle were pierced by the doors and a few small windows of the rooms attached to the outer wall. Four horses stood saddled at a rail at one side. The men who had opened and closed the gate and the stock tenders drifted over to look at him.

'How does a man get to El Paso from here?' Harry asked.

The station keeper wore round, rimless glasses, and his expression was patient and kindly. 'He either waits for the stage—assuming there is another—or he rides or walks. Whether he rides or walks, the next stage will pass him before he gets there; so he might as well have waited here in safety.'

'How far is it?'

The old man said slowly, 'Three hundred and seventy miles.'

'I've got to get there,' Harry said. 'And I can't wait three days to start.'

'I'm sorry,' said the old man.

'What about Bird?' one of the stock tenders suggested.

'Who's he?' Harry asked quickly.

'Allen T. Bird,' said the station keeper thoughtfully. 'I doubt it. He's a company vet,' he told Harry. 'He's overdue, and I've given up on him. Allen travels up and down between Fort Chadbourne and El Paso. Depending on whether or not he has any sick animals to treat, he might get you there faster than walking, or he might not. But he has a two horse wagonette and he moves right along. Allen T. Bird, the mad veterinary of the Overland Mail. Are you interested in phrenology, poetry, or the alimentary disorders of large animals?'

'No,' Harry smiled. 'But I could try to be.'

'If Allen comes along, I think you'd better try. Come in and have something to eat.'

Harry told Hansford, the mail agent, his story while the old man prepared supper.

Afterwards they ate in the dirt-floored room which was part kitchen and part dining-room. Outside, an evening wind whipped dust at the windows. Sooty pots hung from cranes above a fire. Pans hung against the walls, a churn rested beside the fireplace and a German clock on the mantelpiece told the hour in a country where even days were unimportant.

'I apologize for the slumgullion,' said the old man. 'My wife and the other ladies have been sent back to Fort Chadbourne. Too much going on just now.'

Harry carried in the blankets from the guerrillas' saddle. Inside were packed some eating utensils, a compass, a small clock, and a bottle of Chamberlain's Stomach and Liver Tablets. He gave the clock and liver tablets to Hansford. Hansford dragged a straw pallet up near the fireplace and told Harry to make his bed there.

In the morning Harry helped with watering and feeding the stock. Then he carefully groomed Captain Thomas's grey, hunting faults in the gelding and trying to decide whether it was safe to start out on this horse in case the veterinary did not get through. It was a clean-limbed, powerful animal, and should be able to carry him thirty miles a day for a few days without suffering. Thirty miles a day would get him to El Paso in about twelve days, if he lived.

And while he inched along through West

Texas, Canty would have the run of things. Most likely he would put Lute underground first, and that was all right with Harry. But then he would go to work on Kelsey. Given a free hand, Canty probably had a whole closetful of nasty little tricks for getting information out of young women.

Harry threw the corn brush at the tack box and walked into the screened room behind the kitchen, where Hansford was cutting up an antelope haunch.

'Mr. Hansford,' he said. 'I'm going to try it.'

'All right, son. Probably it's best.' Hansford wiped his hands on his apron.

'It's hard to explain why I've got to get there, but I do. If the horse gives out, I can probably make a swap at one of the stations.'

'It'll be a losing game—a good horse and a few dollars for a bad horse. After a few swaps—Still, who can say which game will lose you most? Maybe that stage yesterday was the last westbound we'll ever see. I'll shake up a bait of food for you,' he said.

'I can't pay,' Harry mentioned. 'They cleaned me out.'

'You've already paid,' said Hansford. 'Those liver pills were just what I've been needing.'

A voice seeming to come from the wall boomed hollowly, 'Mr. Hansford. Horsebackers a mile east.'

Hansford stooped quickly before a round corner fireplace. 'Coming up, Will,' he

98

shouted.

Harry strode after him to the rack of guns in the main room, took the short-barrelled revolving rifle he handed him, looped powder and ball flasks about his neck, and followed to a ladder outside. Four men were running up pole ladders to the roof of the big hollow square building. From behind the parapet wall they surveyed a landscape the hue of a russet potato, patterned with wintry mesquite thickets like dried moss and areas of coarse yellow grass. Across the north marched a line of hills like peaks pinched up out of wet clay. The men stood gazing at a thin banner of dust rising from the scraggly grey jungle and drawing near.

As a two-horse team pulling a topped wagon appeared in the distance, Hansford chuckled, 'There's your man. That's Bird.'

*     *     *

Pulling off long yellow gauntlets, the veterinary passed behind the line of horses standing cross-tied beneath a thatch of higar cane. He laid a hand on the rump of a dapple grey. 'This'n,' he said to the hostlers. He singled out three more and all were led to a hitching rail. Bird took a file and went to work on the teeth of one animal. He was a tall, sturdy man of sixty who wore a brown duster with leather elbows. His hat was a black felt

99

with a round crown, and there was a pink desert flower fixed to the brim of it. His eyes twinkled behind goggling spectacles.

When Bird finished, Hansford said, 'This man's got to get to El Paso, Allen. Name of Harry Logan. Will you take him?'

Glancing quickly at Harry, the veterinary took a can of hoof ointment from his wagonette and began doctoring hoofs. 'You from Illinois?'

'Missouri.'

'There was a family by that name in Sibley, near where I was raised. Why in the world did you leave Sibley?' Bird asked curiously.

'I'm from Missouri,' Harry smiled.

'I like the desert,' Bird conceded, 'but I wouldn't trade one square block of Sibley for a hundred miles of Texas. A Texan will tell you there's good parts and there's bad parts—but I reckon you're proud of every square inch of Sibley, ain't you?'

'His home's in Missouri, Allen,' said Hansford uncomfortably. 'Have you got room for him?'

The veterinary stared thoughtfully at Harry. He asked some questions, and decided finally that Logan might make a suitable travelling companion. In fact, he welcomed someone to talk to. It was a fact that he talked to the horses so much that they had memorized several lines of his poetry. It would be a pleasure; but he could predict nothing about when they might arrive in El Paso. The vibrations in the earth under his head last night had been rather ominous.

## CHAPTER ELEVEN

One evening four days after Harry Logan was left with Thomas's guerrillas, Pete Canty and the hollow-eyed survivors of the stage journey reached El Paso. Including the usual way-passengers there were fifteen of them. In the dusky stage yard behind the big mail agency, they were greeted sombrely by the division superintendent, a short, powerful, irritable-appearing Irishman with a florid face and yellow hair. His eyes were sharp and blue under bleached brows.

'I expect you know by now this is the end of the line,' he said. 'Temporarily; maybe for good. Colonel McCurdy, at the fort, promises a military escort as soon as possible. For the time being you'll be residents of El Paso.'

He smiled faintly. God help you, the smile said.

Laymon Russell raised his hand. 'If there are rooms to rent,' he said quickly, 'I'd like to put in my bid for two for my daughter-in-law and myself.'

'The last rooms,' said Woodsun, the superintendent, 'went by lot to the last batch of passengers. All I can offer you is a shakedown in the coaches you see standing in the sheds.'

Canty interrupted Russell's hard-tongued complaint. 'Did some people named Geary come in? I missed connexions with them in Missouri. We're friends.'

'They're staying here. Ask at the office for the numbers of their rooms.'

'What about meals?' asked Judith Russell.

Softening a little, Woodsun said, 'The Shoo-Fly restaurant is my choice. I wouldn't go venturing into any of the Mexican cafés. Aside from food, I've got three words of advice for you, and bear in mind that this town is as crowded as seven Swedes in a porch swing. Number one: Wherever you eat, never eat a raisin until it's had a chance to fly away. Number two: Stay on this side of the river. The Mexican village across the way was originally laid out as one of the lower levels of hell; but they decided it was too tough even for a sinner. Number three: If anybody tries to sell you passage on a stagecoach, horse, boat or balloon that'll get you to California, keep your hands in your pockets. Nobody's going in any direction except east—and I'm not sure yet when that'll be.'

After digesting the welcoming speech, Canty learned the numbers of the Harpers' rooms at the stage office on the plaza. Marshal Lindsay looked at the badge Canty exhibited and read his credentials. He was a thin, hard, little man with sandy moustaches and two revolvers. Somehow in all the chaos he managed to look neat and efficient in a grey suit and fancy double-breasted waistcoat. He handed the letters back to Canty.

'Is it sympathy or congratulations you want?'

'Neither. All I want is co-operation.'

'In what respect?'

'There are two fugitives from justice staying at the stage station—a train robber-murderer and his sister. She's wanted, too. I'd like them jailed until I can get them extradited to Missouri.'

'In the first place,' the marshal said, 'you may be a train robber yourself, for all I know. In the second place, the jail is full. I've got room only for qualified felons of my own.'

Canty waited angrily until he was sure the marshal was finished. 'Thanks,' he said. 'I know where I stand, now.'

'That's quite a bit in itself,' said the marshal. 'I'm sorry I can't be more sympathetic, but I've been right busy. Every morning I turn over six or eight deserters to the fort. Every day I have to break up knife fights among the mule-skinners in the plaza and fist fights among the bullwhackers. At night I carry dead gamblers out of the saloons and stop the girls from clawing out each other's eyes.'

'Get paid for it, don't you?' Canty asked.

'Not if I get killed.'

'I'm doing my work out of charity, Marshal. I paid for my own ticket even. All I get when I make Missouri with these people is my old job back.'

'Is it worth it?' asked the marshal, smiling.

Canty squeezed his fist with his other hand, as though he were cracking walnuts. 'It is to me,' he said.

He strolled the dusty, firelit plaza where in the cool autumn evening teamsters were cooking supper, and oxen and mules were being tended and cursed in two languages. Four lines of low-roofed adobe structures bounded the plaza with dirt walks in front of them, and at intervals along the walks a dusty desert cedar or an occasional red fire barrel. The stage station with its arcaded walk occupied half of the south side of the plaza. Suddenly a shot sounded. A moment later Marshal Lindsay emerged from his office and walked towards the west, where the greatest concentration of saloons appeared to be. *The iron terrier*, thought Canty. *I hope they've got a shot left for you.*

For now that he had his 'coons treed, he could not take them without running into trouble with the local law.

While his mind was grinding on it, he saw a man and woman appear from the main entrance of the stage depot. A silken heat went through Canty. Standing beside the tree, he watched the young woman move quickly east and turn the corner, while the man lit a cigar, threw the match in the road, and started across the plaza. Canty waited until he knew it was Lute Harper. Then he moved behind a tree. *Not yet, not yet*, he lectured himself. Not with the iron terrier on the job in El Paso. Somewhere on a side street, after he had been through Harper's luggage. Not until he had found the money or gotten out of the girl where it was hidden.

Harper strolled through the plaza, carelessly but watchful, his head looking large for his long, thin frame. Canty was close enough to see his malarial face and the fringe of yellow beard following the line of his jaw. Lute Harper reached the west end of the square and entered a saloon.

Canty returned to the stage station. Avoiding the office, where he heard Russell arguing about a room, he moved through an arched passage to the patio enclosed by the inner walls of the sleeping rooms. The adobe walls, with their scabs of old plaster, ascended to parapet roofs from which stubby beams and wooden drains protruded. Drifts of brown and yellow leaves from the cottonwoods growing along the streets had collected against the walls. Canty stood against the wall, humming to himself. Soon he could make out the room numbers on the wall at his right. Eleven and twelve were his lucky numbers and he deduced that they would be diagonally to his right, in the corner. He was correct. The doors were locked and the shutters on the windows pulled to, but he was able to open one with his pocket-knife. Then he slit the mosquito-bar screen, glanced about the patio, and climbed into the room.

Canty went through the girl's luggage first, working by the ruddy light of a small mesquite-root fire. Everything she owned, which was virtually nothing, was packed neatly in a new tin suitcase. Probably she had purchased it in Fort Smith, Arkansas. The suitcase contained some garments, a book, and a bag of sachet. But there was not one note of the stolen currency.

Canty inspected the mattress. It contained nothing more significant than some limp swamp-hay stuffing. He swore to himself and went to gaze out the window. From time to time someone would pass from the corral to the front or to one of the rooms. He stepped through the window again and forced his way into Harper's room. He found little of significance there except a powder-flask, and he poured the powder from it on to the kindling in the little oven-like fireplace, against the moment when Lute dropped a match into the kindling. But if Harper had brought any of the money with him, it was on his person at this moment.

Canty swore bitterly and left the room by

the window. How soon would Lute know the stage had come in? Or did he know it now? Time was sputtering out like a short fuse. *All right*, he decided, *I'll go back to where I wanted to start—the girl.* Sooner or later, here or on the way back to Missouri, she would decide to dictate a statement. It might take persuasion, but he viewed it as digging for gold he knew was there. And that statement and the girl's story in court would jail her, hang Lute Harper, and if Harry Logan ever talked his way out of Captain Thomas's clutches, hang Logan beside him.

He re-entered her room and drew the shutters so that she would not suspect he was there until she entered. Lute, he hoped, was launched on some serious drinking for the evening. Canty took the book from the girl's suitcase and sat near the fire to look at it. 'My God, poetry!' He threw it on the bed.

The whole damn trouble with the world today, he decided, was that women were beginning to think they were somebody. They read magazines and poetry and attended temperance meetings. Whereas the fact was that women were women. Certain distinct talents were theirs, one of which was not thinking; another of which was not skipping custody in Missouri and landing in Texas smelling like a rose.

By the very nature of things, women were parasites, incapable of making their own way.

So they must coax, trap or browbeat some male into shouldering their freight. He had little doubt at this moment that the Harper girl, with her innocent blue eyes, had put together the whole crime by which the Harper gang had hoped to live on the fat for ever after.

There was little anyone could tell Pete Canty about women. He knew all about them before he was ten, watching them spin their dinky little webs in his father's saloons. There were good and there were bad; the good ones were the ones who had not found it necessary to be bad.

Canty's need for women was frequently compelling, but it did not blind him to its nature. In no sense did it approach religion or worship. It was merely a pulse-thumping, singing-in-the-ears excitement like the kind that started a man drinking or looking for a fight.

Suddenly he heard footsteps coming from the street. He came silently to his feet. A person walked as distinctively as he did anything else, and Canty had a good ear: It was the girl's tread, sure enough. And he did not hear Lute's sauntering stride through the steady tap of her heels. He heard her step through some dry cottonwood leaves and approach the door. Canty's whole being nettled pleasurably as she stopped and apparently began hunting her key in her purse.

Metal scraped lightly, the lock turned, the door opened and she came inside. She turned her back to him to extricate the key from the lock and insert it into the other side of the door. She was a well-set-up woman, slender and not too hippy, and when she turned a bit her profile was like the face on a coin, and her bosom was just full enough for him.

'Good dinner?' asked Canty softly. Her handbag dropped, and she screamed. Canty bounded to her and slapped his hand over her mouth. 'Damn you, shut up!' He jammed her against the door and held her there, listening. He had forgotten that a woman never got too scared to scream; it was as instinctive as the bristling of a cat's back. But the walls were three feet thick and it was silent outside. She was trying to bite his hand, and he yanked it away and held his doubled fist menacingly. She was fragrant of the same lavender sachet he had found in her suitcase. Suddenly she looked as though she might slump to the floor. Canty watched her. She was breathing very deeply with her eyes closed.

'That's better,' said Canty. 'Where's your brother?'

Her eyes opened and she looked at him steadily. 'He went to drink somewhere. Do you want him or me?'

'I'm coming to that. When'll he be back?'

'Late, if he runs true to form. Where is Harry?' she asked.

'Be quiet. Where's the money?'

'I don't know—I don't know! You don't believe me, of course, but I don't know whether he brought it along or not.' Her face was thin and pretty in the firelight. Her hair, brushed till it glistened, was drawn back to a knot low on her head.

'What do you mean you don't know?' Canty scoffed, taking her by the shoulder. 'That's a pretty good bundle of paper to slip inside a man's shirt, ain't it?'

'It's in a long metal box, but it might be in the suit-case Lute bought at Fort Smith. We stayed in an old cabin one night, and he might have hidden it somewhere there.'

He could feel her shoulder flinch from his grip. He released her and his eyes burned blackly into hers. 'I went through his stuff and it's not there.'

'Then it's either in Missouri or he's carrying it with him.' Standing against the door, Kelsey hugged herself. 'I've told you all I know. Now will you tell me where Harry is?'

Canty's mouth spread into a grin. 'We left him in the brush about four hundred miles back. Some Rebs stopped us and took most of our money and weapons. They stole Harry off us, too.'

She stared at him. 'Why did they take him?'

'Reckon they liked his looks. Maybe they were going to barbecue him. Couldn't say.'

Kelsey bit her lip, then said, 'I could help

you. But I won't unless you tell me the truth about Harry Logan.'

'How could you help me? Little piece of fluff like you.'

'I could help you catch Lute. I could call him in here after he comes back, and you could trap him. You want him alive, don't you?'

'For a while . . . All right,' Canty said soberly. 'This is the pure quill.' And he told her about the kidnapping, omitting his part in it. 'He'd given his money belt to a girl on the stage to keep for him, figuring they wouldn't search her. But they must have reckoned his loose change wasn't all he had, so they held him. They'll let him go, I expect.'

Her frown was a queer one. 'He gave his money to a girl?'

Canty pinched her cheek. 'Don't never fret over a stage man, honey. Ficklest men in the world. I tell you where this girl slept all the way from Burnsville—on Harry's shoulder.'

'Where is the girl?' asked Kelsey quietly.

'Looking for a room here in town, I suppose. If I was you, I'd set myself to get square with him. I'm kind of a specialist on women, and I pick you for one that needs lovin' comfort plumb regular. Am I right?'

Kelsey slipped from the door as though to pass to the fireplace, but Canty caught her wrist and pulled her to him. Smiling lazily into her eyes, he saw her fright.

'Let me go,' she said. Her colour was heightened, the pupils of her eyes were huge.

'Business, business,' sighed Canty, taking her by the waist and shaking her playfully. Then, with a yank, he brought her to him, stifling her cry with his mouth. He locked her against him with one arm while his free hand cupped the back of her head and forced her lips hard against his. She writhed and thrust at his shoulders and, giving that up, scratched his neck. Canty grunted and thrust her away. With one hand he slapped her face.

'You're a Harper, all right,' he rapped, and gave her a shove towards the bed. She fell on it but twisted quickly to sit up and face him.

'If I was you I'd think about working with me, instead of against me. I talked to the marshal, and he wanted to lock you up. I got him to put it off until I'd had a chance to talk to you.'

She was pale and rigid. 'Well, you've talked to me.'

'But I haven't got much out of you, have I?'

'All right, tell the marshal,' the girl invited.

Canty fenced with ideas. 'I reckon it's about come to that. They've got two cells over there, one for women and one for men. Both of them full. The ladies will tear the clothes right off of you, honey, if they think they can wear 'em.'

Out in the patio a man was walking through the leaves, humming to himself. Canty straightened. Boots approached the corner of

112

the patio where the girl's room was. Kelsey's hands clenched the bed-clothing; and Canty then knew for sure it was Lute.

'Will he come in here?' he asked quickly.

'He may.'

'Listen! You're going to help me take him, or I'll kill you both. I want him alive and talking.' He was speaking rapidly, thinking ahead. He gazed around the room. 'When he comes, let him in. I'll be behind the door.'

As he spoke he watched her mouth. She bit her lip in some indecision. 'Trying to decide between me and him,' Canty thought. 'Maybe Lute's been giving her trouble too.'

'I mean it about killing you,' he added. 'Don't try to trick me.'

A key scraped in the escutcheon of the door next to Kelsey's. She looked up, her features in control. 'I won't trick you. He tried to kill Harry. But I hate both of you.'

The door opened and shut. Through the deep adobe wall, no sound passed from Luther's room. Canty stepped to Kelsey's door and unlocked it. At the same time, he heard the other door reopen.

'Sis?' Lute whispered tensely at the door.

Canty drew his Colt and indicated with a gesture where Kelsey was to stand. He placed himself in the corner behind the door, so that when it was opened he would be hidden. 'Answer him,' he whispered.

'What is it?' called the girl, standing there in

the middle of the floor.

'That coach came in,' said Lute. 'Seen anybody?' His hand was trying the latch now, and finding the door unlocked, pushed it open. Canty held his breath, the gun raised like a hatchet. He watched Kelsey who stood straight as a candle. *Move a little*, Canty's fierce scowl warned. *He's going to wonder.*

'The driver was in the saloon,' Lute said, standing in the doorway but not coming in. He seemed to have orders about respecting her privacy. 'Wouldn't tell who was on the passenger list. He was hunting rooms for them. Hear anything?' he asked.

'Yes,' said the girl. 'Come in and I'll tell you what we have to do.'

Canty heard him stir, heard a coin jingle, then a catch of breath. 'Who's been here? There's a smell—' He was like an animal, all his senses whetted.

All at once Lute was backing out of the room. His hand caught the edge of the door and yanked, and as it banged closed Canty heard him running across the patio. He tore the door open and rushed outside. The tall, angular frame of Lute Harper was sprinting towards the gate at the back which opened on the stage yard. Canty levelled his gun. The huge, shattering roar and flash were so powerful that the walls limiting the patio seemed to crack. Lute crashed into the gate. He cried out. Canty took a stride forward and

114

placed himself behind a switch of a cottonwood tree. He could see nothing but lights after the yellow-orange explosion. But he could hear men shouting somewhere, and people in the rooms of the station were crying out. A hinge creaked. The gate banged and Canty started after Lute. Then he stopped, as someone moved into the arched *zaguán* and bawled, 'What the hell was that?'

Canty dropped back to the door of Kelsey Harper's room. He was afraid of walking into Lute, afraid of being hauled in for killing or attempting to kill him, yet afraid of losing him, too. But there was nothing to do but wait and try to find him later. He closed the door.

For a while he could hear Superintendent Woodsun and two or three men poking about the patio, asking questions of each other in loud voices. 'Should I get the marshal?' asked one of the men finally.

'Let me do the thinking,' snapped Woodsun. 'As long as they carry out their own dead around here, I'm not of a mind to stew over shots in the night. Trouble! I reckon it was invented on a stage line!'

'Did you hit him?' asked Kelsey. Outside there still were running feet and voices shouting questions, but it would soon die down, Canty knew. In this town a shooting was normal. 'I winged him,' he said. 'I hope he rots. But not before I find him. I'll stay here a while and then take his room.'

                        *        *        *

'Injuns or guerrillas, one or the other,' said
Allen Bird grimly.

A few hundred feet off the road, the
veterinarian's wagon was hidden in a snarl of
screwbean mesquite. He and Harry were
standing on the wheels while they peered
north-west. Harry could see the smear of
smoke against the foot of a mesa a few miles
away.

'Sure it's Stillwell's Station?' he asked.
'Might be a freighter's camp.'

'It's Stillwell's, all right. Might nice feller he
was, too. Salt of the earth. Hope it was quick
for him.'

Shaking his head, he began to climb down.

'Now, wait,' Harry suggested. 'Maybe he's
just burning off some brush around the station
so nobody can Injun up on him.'

'He burned the brush last month. Old
Stillwell's quit, no doubt about it. We've got to
swing wide around that'n. If it's guerrillas, they
may know my habits. Might be waitin' for me.
All this equipment would be plumb valuable to
a gang of horsebackers.'

Sighing, he took up the lines and led the
horses back to the trace they had followed
from the mail road. Harry felt the hard lash of
desperation. A detour would mean many
hours lost.

                        116

'Maybe they need help, Mr. Bird!' he protested. 'Besides, if the station's burned, it must mean they've left.'

Bird did not discuss it further. Having led the team around, he climbed to the seat again and they started due south.

## CHAPTER TWELVE

Some time after Canty left, Kelsey heard him moving into Lute's room with his baggage. She had become numb. Sitting in the tiny lamplit room, she gazed into the fire. She did not trust Canty, and his story about Harry's abduction sounded too convenient. Then did it mean Harry had been killed by Canty on the trip west?

An enormous need for something took over her feelings. Settledness—that was all she could call this need of hers: The ability to believe that at least some things were established. Nothing but uncertainty had been true in Kelsey's life. She hardly remembered her father. She recalled a number of small, depressing rooms where she and her mother had lived after his death. Rooms in relatives' homes and boarding houses, and the last terrible home of all, with the Harpers. She whispered Harry's name to herself, almost in a sort of prayer.

There was a tapping at the door. She waited until it was repeated.

'Who is it?'

'You don't know me,' a girl's voice said. 'If you're Kelsey Harper, I have some news for you.'

Kelsey opened the door and the light caught the face of a dark-haired girl somewhat shorter than she, with smooth, olive-tinged features and dark eyes. She wore a cape over her shoulders.

'I'm Kelsey Harper,' Kelsey said.

The girl brought a small parcel from beneath her cape. There was a stir of motion near the passageway to the plaza. A man was standing there.

'You might tell me who your friend is,' Kelsey said.

'It's just my father-in-law,' said the girl. 'I'm Judith Russell. I was with your friend, Harry Logan, on the stage that came in tonight. May I come in?'

Kelsey let her in. 'Where is Harry?' she asked quickly.

Judith warmed herself at the fire. 'I wish I knew. We were stopped by some men who said they were Confederate soldiers. They held Harry back.'

'It's true, then. A man who was on the stage with you told me the same story.'

Judith smiled. 'I wouldn't believe much that Pete Canty told me, Kelsey. But you can believe that. Probably he didn't tell you, though, that he put a letter in Harry's pocket that the men found. That was why they held him. And there's another thing he couldn't have told you because he didn't know it. I put a gun in Harry's pocket just before they took him away.'

Kelsey was startled, not certain whether a pocket pistol was a good idea. 'I wonder if he would try to use it?'

'If I know Harry, he'll make the most of any opportunity,' Judith said in the smug way in which some women spoke of men they liked.

'Thank you for helping him,' Kelsey said.

Judith handed her the parcel. 'This is his money belt. I hid it for him while they were searching us. They didn't search the ladies.'

Feeling the solid weight of the small package, Kelsey wondered: *Then why don't I feel more grateful? Because I'm jealous of her,* she decided. Because Judith Russell also looked like a person who would make the most of her opportunities.

'Do you want to do something for me now?' Judith asked.

'Of course.'

'I'd pay the rent if I could share your room with you. There isn't a room unrented in this whole town.'

'I'd be happy,' Kelsey said, thinking of Canty. 'It's even possible Mr. Canty might let your father-in-law share the room next to me.

He was able to get it away from the man who had it.'

Ten minutes later Kelsey heard the Russells talking to Canty. To her surprise, she heard Canty gruffly accept.

\*     \*     \*

Kelsey wondered what direction Canty's edged cruelty would take now. But for the next two days he played a waiting game. He came and went quietly, and left her alone. In the restaurants, she listened for gossip about the shooting, and watched for Lute everywhere.

On the third day Judith came excitedly into the room and sat on the bed. 'There's a stage leaving Wednesday night!'

Kelsey was brushing her hair. She stopped with the brush raised. 'For California?'

'For San Antonio and the Gulf. There are clippers from Indianola to California, and even a steamship to New Orleans. Isn't it wonderful? The commandant at Fort Bliss has finally promised us an escort. It may be the last stage out.'

'I don't know . . .'

'You mean you can't afford it? The Butterfield company will refund your money, and the San Diego and San Antonio mail will give us preference. If you're still short—'

'No, I mean—well, I can't leave until I know about Harry.'

Judith was silent. At last she looked up. 'Kelsey—I don't know how to tell you—'

Kelsey almost knew what she was going to say. 'What is it?'

'Harry's dead, dear.'

Kelsey heard the brush strike the floor. 'Oh, no!'

'After those men let the stage go, I looked back. I saw—I saw them stand him at the edge of the road and fire at him.' Suddenly she put an arm about Kelsey's shoulders. 'Oh, I'm so sorry. I wish I were mistaken. But—'

'You are mistaken! You told me the same thing Canty told me before.'

'But that's all Canty saw. I was facing the back and I could see it. Kelsey, he had me read your letter to him at Fort Smith, so I know how much you need him. But he's gone now. You must realize it.'

'Are you going?' Kelsey asked.

Judith shrugged. 'I hope so. Father and I are still fighting it out. He's determined to wait and go on to San Francisco by stage. I'm just as determined to go home. Don't try to decide now. Tomorrow will be time enough.'

*She's lying*, Kelsey thought as Judith went out. She had said the same thing Canty did before. Yet it could be true. How could she know?

# CHAPTER THIRTEEN

Allen T. Bird got interested in the excellent time he was making between Hansford's and El Paso, and he cut two minor stations completely rather than slow down. In that way they made up part of the time lost on the detour. They were seven days on the road, but he had given Harry little time to fret. He had kept him occupied with half-mad commentaries on life and love; a core of fine sense was in him, but also he was undeniably crazy.

Near dusk of that last day they passed through a pleasant river valley of vineyards and ranches. The Rio Grande lay on their left, a muddy stream in a wide, sandy bed between low cliffs. Smoke and dust softened the sunset ahead of them. An hour later they passed a long earth dam, where the water had been penned and utilized by mills at either side of the river. Due south over a road crossing the dam was Paso del Norte, the Mexican town. Bird turned straight north into the town of El Paso, a mile away.

The tired team shuffled along through the dust and smoke. They passed a pole-and-brush shelter like a chicken roost, beside which was a canvas sign, *New Mesquite Hotel*. Inside were crude cots in a long line. Ahead, Harry discerned lamplight in the dust.

'Allen, I'll be getting off a few blocks from the depot,' said Harry.

Bird's kindly, bulging eyes peered at him. 'I don't believe you ever told me what you're running away from, did you?'

'I'm not running from anything. I'm trying to catch up.' And then he told Bird about Kelsey and Lute and Canty.

Bird looked up at the sky where the last wash of sunset was drowning in night, gazed down again and said, 'You could wait at the Shoo-Fly restaurant and I'll bring your Kelsey there, if she ain't in custody.'

'Would you do that?'

'Take a table in back—if you can get one. Otherwise wait in the alley. I'll be damned,' Bird frowned, 'if I see how coral can travel from the South Seas to Texas. And it must have come here hundreds of years ago. I've found several pieces of it . . .'

\*     \*     \*

Harry waited inside the restaurant called the Shoo-Fly. There were twenty-odd tables under a fly-specked muslin ceiling. All the tables were taken and people were waiting. Stout Mexican women in full skirts and blouses languidly waited on tables like tired housewives. Among the patrons, Harry saw men in city clothing, cavalrymen from the fort east of town, a couple of cowboys as dark as the leather they wore. Everyone was eating vigorously and talking. Some of the men had maps spread on the tables. Harry went out and looked up the road towards the plaza. Camp-fires burned among the corrals and dusty desert trees, and men came and went before them. The town was swollen with men and animals who had come in over the important trails and been unable to go farther.'

A dark, hollow-cheeked man stopped beside Harry and flapped a tattered stage ticket in his face. 'Here's your ticket out of this hole, friend,' he said. 'There's a coach leaving in the morning for Santa Fe. I had my ticket bought and paid for when a feller hired me to cook for his wagon-train. I paid seventy-eight dollars, but for—'

Harry walked past him. In this town there seemed to be forty men for every woman, and each woman he saw caused him to straighten, and then sag when he saw it was not Kelsey. A wagon headed into the alley where Harry stood, and he moved to let it pass with its load of freshly butchered beef. He frowned again at his watch. Someone called his name. A girl was running across the dark, rutted street towards him. Harry ducked under a hitch-rack and ran to catch her in his arms.

Harry brought her back to the walk at last and they stood close together. She touched his face with her fingertips, and then impulsively kissed him again. 'I'd almost given up,' she said finally. 'Yesterday someone told me you were dead.'

'If I hadn't had a girl on the stage give me her gun, I would have been,' said Harry. He gripped her hands, looking at her.

She looked at him with an odd expression. 'Harry, she was the one who told me you were dead.'

'Judith? Why should she? She took a big chance when she gave me the gun.'

'Perhaps she thought she saw something she didn't. She said when she looked back she saw them fire at you.'

'Maybe she was excited.' Harry drew her back to the mouth of the alley. 'What about Canty and Lute?'

'Canty's around town. He has the room next to me. He tried to capture Lute and he wounded him. I don't know where Lute is or even if he's still alive.'

Harry drew his palm across his brow and felt the grime of alkali and sweat. 'We've got some deciding to do,' he said. 'Are the stages moving yet?'

'No, but there's a special one leaving for some seaport on the Gulf tomorrow.'

'Can you get our tickets tonight?'

'I'll try. Harry, will we keep on running forever?'

'What can we do but run? If we go back we're done. There's a time limit on most

125

crimes, so after a while they can't try us at all.'

'I feel like an animal hiding from the hunters. I think I'd rather be tried and hope to be cleared.'

'If you're tried,' said Harry, 'you won't be cleared.' He leaned against the wall, tired of figuring and cross-figuring and each time coming to a chasm just too wide to jump. 'Where does Canty eat his meals?'

'Here.'

He looked at the street traffic. 'I wouldn't get far with him here. But he's got to be put away while we make that stage.'

Kelsey bit her lip. 'Perhaps with the right bait he could be drawn out of town. He'd risk anything to get Lute.'

Harry thought of the mail road below town. 'Tell him you and Lute had it fixed to meet at Hart's mill if you got separated. The mill's on this side of the river. There's a bench just above the river, below the dam. You can say you were to light a fire there if you wanted Lute. He'd be hiding in the brush. Get him to drive you down.'

'Where will you be?'

'I'll be around. Better tell him you'll make a trade with him. If he promises not to take you back, you'll turn Lute over to him. It'll sound reasonable.'

In the cold, dusty darkness, she clenched her hands. 'What will you do with him then?'

'I'll park him somewhere across the river.

First I've got to catch him. Here—carry this in your handbag. If he gets out of hand, you know how to use it.'

Kelsey took the little revolver.

'I'll make you a trade,' she said. She walked to the alley below the Shoo-Fly restaurant and went a few steps into it. 'Turn your back,' she ordered. He obeyed, and presently she came out carrying his money belt. 'Your friend turned this over to me. I'm glad to be rid of it.' Then she crossed the street and in a short time he had lost her in the traffic. He thought of the sauntering, bitter-eyed man named Canty, and of the advantage held by a man who did not scruple to kill. To kill Canty and roll him in the river: That was easy. But to try to take him alive: That was asking to be killed.


## CHAPTER FOURTEEN

Harry walked down the river and crossed on the dam. Pausing in the middle of it, he gazed at the mill on the American side. An orchard spread from it up the slope, and down river a few hundred yards was the bench where he had told Kelsey to bring Pete Canty. Small mesquite trees and screwbean brush covered it. It was a nice, private place for an ambuscade.

He walked on into the village. The narrow

street smelled sourly and was mined with bog-holes full of slops. There were about two dozen small adobe buildings along the main street, half of them drinking places. Crusts of plaster clung to the adobe walls. Lean dogs sniffed him as he moved down the walk. Somewhere a church bell bonged like a water pipe.

Before a small, and noisy, cantina he stopped to glance inside over blue-slatted doors. He could hear a few American voices in the babble of Spanish, and saw some teamsters at the table playing cards. At the bar were Mexican cowboys in leather pants and jackets and one man dressed like an American in linsey-woolsey trousers, a loose coat, and knee-high boots. He was rolling dice in a solemn, disinterested way with an old man in a big straw sombrero.

Harry went in and stood at the bar next to the men who were rolling dice. They were betting with big Mexican silver pieces and their language was part Spanish and part English. The man who was tending bar came along and set a blue glass before Harry and filled it with milky liquor.

'No beer?' Harry asked.

'No beer, señor,' said the barman. He was probably forty but had faintly withered skin, well-tanned and glossy brown eyes. He had the neat, massaged, dissipated look of a man who has just recovered from a long drunk.

'What's this stuff?' Harry sniffed the liquor. It smelled like sour library paste. 'Haven't you got any whisky or beer?'

'No, señor. One-fifty, please.'

'Give him a dime and throw the stuff in his face,' said the man next to Harry. 'Come on, Paco—the man wants whisky.'

The barman scratched his head. 'Well, I save it for my good customers, Fiero.' But as he spoke he produced a bottle and poured a glass. He stammered a little and blinked rapidly. 'Besides, the—*el hombre atrás bebe casi todo!*'

'Good God, is he still here?' grunted Fiero. He glanced at a narrow, curtained doorway at the end of the bar. Hanging short of the floor, it exposed some sacks against the wall and a tortoise-shell cat sleeping on them.

Harry said to the men who were rolling dice, 'Can I buy you a drink?'

'If you want,' said the man called Fiero. He was short, deep-chested and powerful with immense shoulders. He wore a serious, almost impatient expression. He had quick brown eyes and a healthy brown moustache with a few grey hairs in it. 'Are you stuck over there?'

'Looks that way. I'm hunting a room.'

'So is everybody. Well—*saludos*.' They drank the whisky. Fiero introduced his companion. 'This is Hilario, my boss mule skinner. I didn't get your name.'

'Logan.' Hilario was a man of sixty-some

129

years, with white moustaches and a harelip. They solemnly shook hands.

'Then you're a trader?' Harry asked Fiero.

Fiero twisted his glass. 'Maybe. I was in the Chihuahua trade until last month. With the war going on in your country, I can't get out of town either. You need a room, eh?' he said. *'Paco—ven acá!'*

The barman returned. 'How's the señor in the back?' Fiero asked him.

Paco wrinkled his nose. 'If he stopped drinking, maybe he would go better.'

'Maybe he'd like somebody to look after him tonight.'

Nervously blinking his eyes, Paco stammered, 'No, no! *Madre mia!* He'd kill me if I asked him. You can sleep in one of my chairs,' he assured Harry.

'What's his name?' asked Harry.

'I didn't ask him.'

'What's his name?' Fiero asked him.

Paco leaned forward. 'I know this much. On his bedpost hangs a revolver. On the holster are the letters, *L.H.*'

'I think I know him,' Harry said. 'He's my brother-in-law. He got in a shooting scrape across the river. How is he?'

'He's got a bad leg. He wants a doctor, but there's no doctor in town.'

'Hey, Paco!' a man bawled from behind the curtain.

Paco straightened like a soldier, tucked in

his shirt-tail and walked to the curtained doorway. 'Yes, sir!'

'Is there a doctor out yonder?'

'No, señor—a man was asking *about* a doctor for his wife who is sick.'

'Blast it, you get me a doctor, you ugly little grease-ant! Listen—I want you to carry a letter to El Paso. You got a pencil and paper?'

'Just a minute, *patrón.*'

Harry walked to the rear. He passed through the doorway. At the right was a dark alcove piled with sacks and boxes. A corn-broom slouched against the wall. The cat woke up and stretched. To the left was a hall with some rooms opening off it. Candlelight from the first door was the only illumination. Harry heard someone behind him, and glanced back to see Fiero following. He felt the trader was all right; he was interested in preventing trouble.

He heard Paco stutter, 'Go ahead, *patrón*! I'll take it down.'

Standing in the doorway which had no door. Harry heard a man stirring, heard him mutter to himself and then say drunkenly, *'To Miss Kelsey Harper: This here is a greaser that's been charging me too much rent. Kick his backsides for me. Love, Luther.* That's *L-u-* Wait a minute! Back up. Write this: *I got a bullet in my leg and I need a doctor. Send one over here to—* What the hell—!' he shouted.

Harry had moved into the room, his glance

131

searching for Lute. He saw the bed and started towards it, but an instant later realized Lute was not in it but had moved to a chair. Lute wore his hat, his underwear and one boot and had been speaking as Harry entered, waving a Colt absently as he dictated. Now the long, yellow-bearded skeleton lurched up and levelled the gun as Harry charged. Lute yanked the trigger. Because the Colt was uncocked, it did not fire. He tried to cock it, but just then Harry crashed into him and the gun flashed and roared and the candle was blown out. The bullet struck the dirt floor, glanced into a wall, and hummed about the room like a hornet.

In the darkness they grappled for the gun. There was an odour of sickness about Lute, but he fought like a lynx. The gun thumped on the floor, and in a smoky, snarling fury they searched for it. Harry's hand struck it; he clawed and fumbled as Lute went for it, and finally he was holding it. A light came wavering along the hall as they rose, illuminating Lute's gaunt form. His head looked large for his long, thin frame. Shadows pocketed his cheeks and eye-sockets. Harry could see the dirty bandage about his right calf.

'Sit on the bed, Lute,' he ordered. His heart still sledged at his ribs.

Behind him, the light came up to the door. He heard Fiero sniff the air and say, *'Que caráy!'*

Harry pushed open a shutter to air the room. Powder smoke was thick and choking; the room reeked of infection, liquor and dirty blankets.

'I don't know why I don't kill you,' Harry said. He sat on the chair with Lute's Colt in his underarm holster. Fiero and his mule-boss stood in the room with them.

'I ain't askin' you not to,' said the man on the bed. He lay with his left leg drawn up and his wounded leg limp, his hands under his head. The candlelight dusted his silky yellow beard. An inch long, it traced the curve of his jaws.

'I've got about four good reasons to stamp you out like an ant,' said Harry. 'But I've got a better one to keep you alive.'

'You can't haul me out of this country,' said Lute. 'These greasers ain't about to help you. They been whipped too recent by Uncle Sam.'

Harry caught Fiero's eye. 'Suppose you could find a doctor for this fellow?'

'There's no doctor in El Paso, unless he's travelling.'

Hilario said something in Spanish and Fiero shrugged. 'Well, he isn't really a doctor,' he said. 'He just does some worming. And he treats animals for the stage company. He's taken care of mules for me, too. But he's not in town.'

'Yes, he is,' Harry said. 'Allen Bird? I came

133

in with him tonight. I'll give a dollar to the man who brings him back here.'

'Go get him,' the trader told Hilario. Hilario vanished down the hall.

'How about a drink?' Lute asked.

'You've got enough in your system right now to bottle and cork,' Harry told him. 'You've got company coming, Lute. You want to be all pretty, don't you?'

The sallow face turned. 'Sis?'

Harry smiled. 'Pete Canty.'

Lute's eyes roamed his face.

'You left me for dead, Lute. You pushed Kelsey across the line with you and God knows where *that'll* end. I'd like it to end in a small room, just the two of us, and nobody to bat me over the head with a scantling this time. But it can't.' He reached for a short-barrelled rifle leaning against the wall and inspected it.

'You're going to guard him for me, Lute. I'll take him alive, if I can. Then I'll bring him here. You don't look very spry, but I reckon you can hold a gun on a man that's tied up.'

'Me?' Lute said incredulously.

'I'm leaving town tomorrow and I want about three days' start. How'd you like to hold him for me?'

Lute smiled dreamily at the ceiling. 'I'd admire to, friend Logan.'

'You're the best, watchdog I can think of. You're not in shape to follow me yourself, and why should you do him a favour by letting him

134

go? You've already got one of his bullets in you.'

'Talkin' real smart,' Lute said.

'You probably wouldn't kill him either, with so many people around. You're too stove-up to make a run for it if you did kill him. So I figure Canty's chances with you are a sight better than mine were with Captain Thomas. I'll leave money for your board and keep. Or do you have some more of that hard-luck paper money of yours?'

'All gone,' said Lute sadly. 'I got scared and burned it.'

'Bet there's still a little twenty-dollar ash floatin' around. But I'll tell you something, Lute.' Harry drew the Colt and pointed it at him. 'If I ever see you again, I'll use this on you. I'm telling you to stay away from Kelsey and me. If you follow us, I'll know there's no teaching you a thing, and I'll say it next time so you understand. There's a man lying in a gully in Texas who could tell you even Logan can be crowded too far.'

\*       \*       \*

A breeze blew cool and steady as he waited in the mesquite thickets above the dam. From El Paso, the road descended through silvery cottonwoods to the bench on the north bank, where the earth dam was anchored at Hart's mill. Just above the mill was a wagon track into

135

the brush. Deep in the dry and thorny jungle Harry sat beside this road with a coil of rope beside him and listened to a guitar and a singer in the darkness of the Mexican side. It made him lonely. A long and solitary trail had brought him here.

Horses, carts and wagons passed the mill. The road where Harry waited was untravelled. It grew later and chillier. He stood up to flex his muscles. As he did so, he saw the man standing a short distance down-river between the two ruts of the road. His heart struck up hard, and sank and left him shaken. He was uncertain whether he had been seen. The man stepped quickly into the brush at the edge of the road. They were both silent, Harry fading back a yard and slowly sinking to the ground.

He thought desperately, *Now what?* Canty had figured ahead of him, had beaten him here and come alone and from the wrong direction. Canty's gun was cocked and Harry's was muzzled. Harry heard him moving very quietly through the mesquite.

'It's you, ain't it, Logan?' Canty called softly, with a murderous glee in his voice.

Harry picked up the coil of rope. It seemed worthless now. He had planned to rope Canty from the horse or buggy he came on. Looping the rope over his shoulder, he pulled Lute's Colt, a long-barrelled and handsome new weapon. But it was just a testing action to see whether he had the nerve for it, and he dropped it back when he found he hadn't. Why? he wondered. What made Canty any different from Captain Thomas?

What set Canty apart, he concluded, was that in his own way he was an honest man. He was a ruthless, sly falconer in a mailed glove; but the glove was clean. His hatred of men beyond the law was unnatural, but it made him a poor target for a man who held a vision of staying out of jail.

He made a noose in the rope. Very quietly the big, pock-marked man in the brush was coming towards him, foot by foot. Harry began moving along the edge of the road. Canty's progress quickened. Harry tried to understand how Canty's mind was working, what had brought him here in the first place if he suspected a trap. Maybe it was that in El Paso he was as vulnerable, actually, as Harry was. The local law might not back him up. Down here by the river, a man wrote his own laws.

Canty came a little farther, with the painstaking care of a jeweller lifting the hairspring from a watch. He must know the attacker was always the one in the greater danger, Harry reasoned; but the brush was a screen for him as he moved in. Then at the last moment they would be on even terms.

Like a hawk drifting over the brush, the railroad man advanced. Harry glanced around. He must not run out of space to manoeuvre in. To his left the bench swept up sharply to a

137

bank like a high adobe wall. To his right, the mesquite coasted to a cliff dropping fifteen feet to the river. It had looked fairly deep from the dam. Suddenly he heard Canty charging through the brush.

Harry peered in a cold sweat towards the river, and a thought began to spin in him; as the crackling of brush came on he pivoted and broke across the wagon road towards the river.

Canty's gun roared. The flash illuminated the road for an instant. Just then Harry's foot caught under a root and he went down.

## CHAPTER FIFTEEN

As he scrambled up he could hear Canty once more. Again the revolver flashed as Harry went lunging through the fanged brush. He cut to the right and sprawled behind a creosote bush. He drew the Colt and cocked it, gasping for breath. *If I've got to, I've go to*, he decided.

But now Canty halted, too. Patient, dangerous, methodical. Harry put the gun on safety, rose quietly and slipped towards the river. Across the wide stream, in Mexico, the guitarist had ceased playing. At the mill, a man shouted into the night. Once more the hunter was on the move; Harry heard him clear his throat. He drove straight forward.

Suddenly the bench ended like a plank over

a pond. It dropped from beneath him, and he stood there in the breeze gazing at the dark, riffled water fifteen feet below, at sand bars lying like logs in the stream. At the bank's edge there was a small boulder almost ready to fall. He put his boot on it and shoved. As it dropped, he stepped back and crouched behind a squat cactus which resembled a half-opened artichoke with a single, slender branch rising in the centre. Huddling close to it, he waited and snugged the coil of rope about his shoulder. Canty had stopped running; but as the boulder struck the water, he advanced a few feet more before he again halted, listening. Harry tossed a handful of pebbles. They cleared the bank and he heard them stir the water. Still Canty did not move, and Harry raised a larger stone and hurled it like a shotput. As it landed, Canty came cautiously into view, convinced that a man was really down there in the river. From fifteen feet back, he studied the river bank. Harry heard him swear. With his Colt levelled, half crouching, the big man came from the mesquite to the edge of the bluff and stood peering down at the river. His gun swung suddenly to cover something he had apparently seen move. He fired.

At the final instant he heard Harry charging in. He made a back-hand swing with the revolver. Harry struck him in the side, and Canty was lifted from the ground, and hurled forward, so that when he fell there was no ground beneath him. He uttered a short, gasping cry as he dropped. Harry felt earth crumbling under him, twisted and dived for solid ground. Another chunk of earth broke from the bank and Harry's feet went ploughing down the face of the crumbling bank. Only his knees hit but he slid farther down, clawing at the earth, until at last only his arms, fingers and chin were holding him up. He was still holding his revolver. He heard Canty strike the water. Then the earth broke loose and he was falling, too.

The water engulfed him in the darkest, coldest silence in the world. He clawed his way to the air and looked around. He saw a long reach of dark water striped with distant sand bars, turned his head and saw the bank. At the foot of it was a steep three feet of shore. Pete Canty was scrambling on to it. Harry swam a few strokes and caught at his legs. Canty was pulled down, gasping, and Harry dragged him with one hand back into deep water and shoved his head under. He pushed Canty like a log into the slow currents of the river, turned and struggled from the stream and shook the water from his pistol. Chagrined, he looked at it. He tried a testing shot into the water near Canty; the hammer fell, the priming-cap cracked, a prolonged fizzling sound and a great quantity of smoke came sputtering out. Harry holstered the gun and looked for a piece of driftwood.

He found it just as Canty was wallowing back to shallow water. He shoved the jagged end of the mesquite branch at his face and Canty slipped and went under. He was gagging when he came up. He waved an arm at Harry.

'*Can't swim!*' he gasped.

Harry remembered the hard, wet coil still about his shoulder. As Canty struggled into shore, Harry rammed the pole into the side of his head. Canty fell back again, floundering. When he waded in again, Harry offered him the pole. Seizing it, Canty feverishly pulled himself towards the narrow strip of wet land.

Canty stood on the tilted ledge with him, dripping and winded, staring gauntly and thrusting both hands back over his black hair to run the water from it. In a sudden violent effort he swung at Harry's head. The blow glanced off his ear and Canty rolled a roundhouse swing at his jaw. Turning his head, Harry felt it pass, and then braced himself flat-footedly and dug a short blow to Canty's ribs. Already winded, the railroad man coughed and hunched his shoulders. Harry chopped one to his nose and Canty snorted, blood and water streaming over his mouth and chin. He slammed his head down and it hit the bridge of Harry's nose. Chips of light exploded in Harry's head. Canty was throwing both fists then and ramming Harry against the cliff. But his power was that of nerves, not muscles, and

Harry covered up and waited them out.

As the big man slowed, Harry hurled him off and set himself. His shoulders rolled in the motion of a man chopping wood, and his fists flashed to Pete Canty's jaw, landing jarringly and with a sweet shock that rippled all the way to his shoulder. Canty went back and landed spread out in the water and rolled over like a log.

Harry dragged him ashore and tied his hands, bound his arms to his torso and waited for him to recover consciousness.

\*        \*        \*

Allen T. Bird was driving his Overland Mail wagon from the village towards the dam when Harry and Pete Canty came walking up the main street of Paso del Norte. Harry followed Canty closely with a length of mesquite for a weapon.

'Whatta you got there, boy?' Bird exclaimed. 'It looks like a man, but it drips like a fish.'

'This is a friend from Missouri. He's going to stay with Lute a while. How's my friend Lute?'

'If I had that leg,' Bird said, 'I wouldn't be seen dead with it. But I had them hold him down and I cleaned it out and left a piece of string through the hole to keep it open and draining.'

142

'Is he conscious?'

'Oh, yes. And looking forward to some company he said you were bringing him.'

'Will you wait for me?' Harry asked. 'I'll be done in fifteen minutes.'

'Do you think you'll get away with this?' Canty asked as they went towards the cantina.

'Get away with what? I'm giving you the same chance you gave me with our friend Brown.'

'The chance to be killed by Lute Harper instead of you? With Brown you had a chance to jaw your way out of it.'

'Lute knows the way the law works out here. They'd probably stand him against the wall and shoot him if he killed you. And he's in no shape to travel. You're just going to bunk with him a few days.'

Canty walked into the saloon. Behind the little bar Paco was laughing with a customer and blinking in his nervous manner. Seeing Harry, he became suddenly sober. 'Straight through the little door,' growled Harry. Canty ducked through the curtain and Harry pushed him towards Lute's door.

Propped up in bed, Lute was waiting. 'Welcome, Brother Canty,' he said. 'Anything you want and don't see, just ask for it.' His face was tallow-coloured, hardly darker than his yellow teeth.

'I don't see you dead yet, but I can wait,' said Canty. He stared around the small cavelike room with its raw mud walls, its disorder and hopelessness. Then he sniffed. 'God, wherever there's a Harper, there's a stench.'

Lute blinked like a sunning lizard. 'Wherever there's a bullet, there's rot.'

'There's rot in your mind,' Canty told him. 'I'd rather be dead with a clean guard than alive with a Harper.'

Harry sat Canty in the chair. He found Lute's powder and ball flasks and began reloading the Colt. His coat was wet and warm and he pulled it off.

Harry found manacles in Canty's pocket and locked one of Canty's ankles to the frame of the bed. Then he removed the rope. During this operation, Canty's gaze followed him with concentrated savagery. As Harry flipped the rope away, the detective rose swiftly and snatched his Colt. When Harry twisted clear Canty threw a savage blow that crashed against his head. Harry stumbled back and Canty swung a long overhand blow that missed. Harry shook his head and stared at Canty.

Canty grinned. 'I doubt you'll ever see me alive again, Logan, so I wanted you to remember me just this way.'

'Fine,' Harry said grimly, looking at him and then at Lute. 'I'll send a man in with your rifle,' he told Lute. 'Hold him about three days.'

\* \* \*

Harry and the veterinary drove back to the town across the river. In the plaza a fight was going on near a camp fire. A ring of men surged about two bloody combatants who circled each other slowly, one of them armed with a large rock, the other holding a knife. As they drove past the stage station, Kelsey ran down the steps. Harry helped her up on the seat.

She leaned against him, trembling. 'Canty knew it was a trap. He said we'd leave in a half hour, but he didn't show up. So I knew he'd gone by himself.'

'It's all right. He's staying with Lute. We're all set,' Harry said with a long sigh. 'Tomorrow we'll be on that stage.'

Kelsey gazed at him hopelessly. 'No, Harry. Not tomorrow. Maybe not ever.'

'What's the matter?' Harry asked. And that cold, vacant feeling came back to him.

'The trip's been cancelled. The commandant at the fort left this afternoon and took most of the men with him. They think he's gone to join the Rebels. There's no escort now, and the superintendent says the guerrillas are active only thirty miles from here.'

Bird peered gloomily at the team as he swung it into the stage yard from the side street. 'I feel like you ought to be out of the way if and when that man gets loose,' he said.

'I feel that way, too,' Harry said.

145

# CHAPTER SIXTEEN

Harry passed the night in the feed barn, wearing dry clothing borrowed from the veterinary. In the morning he asked for Superintendent Woodsun in the office, but was told he had not come from his home yet. 'It's only six,' the clerk told him.

Harry sat on the cold gallery, waiting. In the smoky, cluttered plaza, half-dressed men yawned and scratched as they moved about. A few fires were burning. From a tall tree, a congregation of large, naked-headed turkey buzzards flapped off, one by one, to the day's work. Men lay on blankets beneath wagons and beside dead camp fires; men sat on boxes staring at nothing. Barn sour, thought Harry, sick of town and idleness. But they can't go anywhere. They'll keep on fighting until there's nobody left to fight.

At seven o'clock, a short, red-faced, irritable looking man walked towards the office entrance. Harry moved quickly to stand in his way.

'Mr. Woodsun? My name's Logan. I was wondering—'

The blue eyes crackled. 'You were wondering if you could sell me a ticket, or buy a ticket, or rent a room or—'

'No, sir, I've already got a ticket. But I

heard the run to San Antonio had been cancelled for lack of an escort. Well, why not raise our own?'

'Don't talk to *me* about escorts,' retorted Woodsun. 'I was on the last coach through Apache Pass last month. We had a civilian escort, Logan. Eleven men who scattered like quail at the first yip of an Apache. We outran everything including the escort, or I'd be wearing my hair on an Indian lance.'

'There's a lot of men in this town who'd like to leave, but are afraid to try it alone,' Harry insisted. 'Why couldn't we organize a mounted force, hitch up all the stages in the yard and take off?'

'Oh, we could,' said Woodsun. 'We could set off with our flags flying, but the first night out somebody'd get a belly-ache, or make love to somebody else's girl, or God knows what, and we'd have a riot. Or if we made it to Van Horn Wells, we'd be out of provisions and boiling up the thoroughbraces. And we couldn't carry enough feed for your mounted miracle men and the sage teams too, though there's more sagebrush and less feed on that San'tone trail than you ever saw. Do you know how far it is to Indianola?'

'I shouldn't wonder if it was over four hundred miles, but—'

'It is eight hundred miles from here,' said Woodsun slowly. 'It is said to be peopled by beings similar to those on earth, but it's so far away nobody seems to be sure. Mister, we can't do one blessed thing without the United States Army. And we just lost it.'

He went into the office, and Harry heard him bellowing, *'Who the hell let this cat sleep on my desk?'*

Someone slipped a hand through Harry's arm. 'That's a lovely flower you're wearing, Harry,' a girl said. 'Did you pick it yourself?'

Harry glanced down at the grey duster of Bird's which he was wearing. A very small blue flower hung from the buttonhole.

'It came with the outfit,' he told Judith Russell. Offering it to her, he said, 'Maybe you'd better wear it. In this town men have been shot for less.'

She put the flower in her hair, gazing at him in a frank and happy way. 'I'm very glad you're back, Harry Logan. Did my little pistol help?'

'If it weren't for your little pistol, I'd still be there.'

'Was it worth a breakfast to you? Your young lady is still sleeping. She won't be out for an hour.'

'She'd better not be, or I might as well be back in the gully with Captain Thomas. Come on.'

She remained close as they walked to the café, holding his arm when they stepped over potholes. He liked her; but you wouldn't believe some of the things she did unless you knew about them firsthand.

'Talk to me, Harry,' she urged.

'I was just trying to figure you out. You might have been shot for giving me that gun. Yet after helping me, you tell people that you saw me killed.'

'I didn't tell *people,* Harry—I just told Kelsey.'

'What's the difference?'

'Well—it's the difference between murder and an act of war. If a civilian shoots a civilian, it's murder. If a soldier shoots an enemy, it's an act of war. This was an act of war.'

'Now I know everything except what you're talking about.' He had an idea, but it might be embarrassing to jump to conclusions.

'I have very strong feelings about you, Harry,' said Judith frankly. 'I think you're a very important chicken in an awfully tough shell. Without help, you may never peck your way out of it.'

Harry smiled. 'I've pecked my way a thousand miles already.'

'A thousand miles towards what?' she said curtly. 'I'm talking about success, not geography. I've known a few rich and important men, like my father-in-law, and except that most of them have inflated themselves like balloons at a county fair, they're really a great deal like you. The big thing about them I've noticed is that they're stubborn. They'll try anything, and usually bring it off. You want to be a big stage

149

operator, and you'll be one. Maybe,' she added significantly.

'I don't know about your big men,' Harry said, 'but I think I know where I'm going.'

'You're not going there with twelve hundred dollars,' said Judith disdainfully. 'That's one road that'll land you in the poor farm before you know it. Do you know how much it costs to build a stage barn or grade a mile of road?'

His shins kicking at the long grey duster, Harry retorted, 'The thing about women is that they all know more about staging than a man who grew up in it.'

Judith put her hand on her hips. 'The thing about men is they're so sure of themselves they don't know hard jobs from impossible ones. Listen to me. My father-in-law is a financier. He and some other men are backing a man named Ben Holladay on a central overland stage route to take the place of this one. I've heard them talk, and I've read his mail. I may not know a singletree from a currycomb, but I do know one thing: You can't operate a stage line without capital.'

Now it was clear why Laymon Russell had argued so confidently that night about staging. He was quiet, and Judith went on, a little subdued, 'If you marry Kelsey, you'll never be more than a hostler around a stage yard. When two people marry, they're both twice as poor as before. Oh, I don't mean to run her down—'

'You just want me to throw her to Canty and a jury and let them tear her apart.'

'When a jury looks into her innocent blue eyes,' Judith assured him, 'she'll probably be in no danger at all. Harry, I've got some money waiting for me in San Francisco in addition to what I'm carrying. I'd like to invest in you.'

'I'm a poor risk.' Harry shrugged.

'But while we've been walking to breakfast you've probably been thinking of ways to make money out of this mess we're in—*if* you had any money.'

Harry gazed down the mean little street leading to Mexico. Everything she said was true. She had been poor long enough to know how a poor man's thinking ran. He said slowly, 'Every good idea I ever had I got trying to sleep in a haystack. You get to itching and listening to the rats, and you can't sleep. So you think. Last night in the hay I had a sure enough idea. I was going to try to buy a couple of coaches and some stock from Woodsun on credit. What's the company got to lose if he sells them? They're sure to be lost if the Rebs take them or some crazy bullwhacker sets fire to the station.'

'Of course,' Judith said. Her tongue moistened her plump lower lip, and she watched his mouth.

'But I decided he'd be afraid the blockade would be broken and the general superintendent would want to know what

151

happened to those coaches. So I gave it up and went to sleep. But when I talked to him this morning I found out something about him. He's afraid of responsibility. He'd duck out if he could.'

Taking his arm again, the girl started him along the walk. 'Maybe after a little more excitement,' Harry said, 'he'll be glad to get out from under.'

'But even if you had the stages,' the girl pointed out, 'they're still a long way from California. And how could you get them there from Indianola?'

'I wouldn't. I'd go north from here and then take one of the wagon roads. There are plenty of scouts and teamsters in this town who'd go along as guides and escorts just to get out.'

After a moment Judith said, 'Harry, I believe we're on our way.'

\*     \*     \*

There was a long counter in the dimly lit stage office room with a map on the wall behind it. The air was smoky with sperm-oil lamps when Harry entered. Five or six pieces of luggage were lined up against the wall near the door, clerks were busy with ledgers and copy work, and at a rolltop desk at the far end of the room Superintendent Woodsun was chewing on a pipe while he listened to a small, erect man with a brown bald head like a rock.

'I don't think it's asking too much of you,' the man was saying. It was Russell.

'Mister, *I* don't care where Canty spent the night,' said Woodsun. 'I don't even care if he comes back. If you're lonesome, find him yourself.'

'But surely you see what I'm getting at? This other man, this Logan, may have waylaid him. I don't like to make accusations, but I do know that Logan is a fugitive from justice.'

All the clerks looked around. 'How do you know?' Woodsun asked.

'Mr. Canty told me about him. He's a peace officer. He should know.'

'Well, you bring Mr. Canty here and let him make his own accusations. In the meantime, if you're the financial genius your letters of introduction say you are, maybe you can tell me how to feed eighty mules and horses on feed for thirty?'

'Sell them to somebody,' said Harry.

Russell did not retreat as Harry came along, but stuck out his chin. 'What happened to Canty?' he demanded.

'He was drunk as a lord last night. Maybe he got in trouble. Why don't you start an investigation?'

Russell snatched his hat from the counter and walked out.

'About those horses and mules,' Harry said to Woodsun. 'Why don't you sell some of them?'

153

'The name is Woodsun, not Butterfield.'

'You're Butterfield's agent, aren't you? Will it help anybody if the animals starve?' He had no real plan yet, but he was throwing some straws in the air.

'No, and it won't help if I sell company property and the stages begin to move again. What do you want with stage animals?'

Harry grinned. 'I was hoping to buy some stages, too.'

The thunder of Woodsun's palm on the desk top resounded in the room. 'Why does every lunatic in El Paso have to come to *my* office to stand on his head and bray like a jackass? I have seventy-two passengers on my hands when I'm prepared for twenty—I can't pay my workmen—I'm down to five days' feed but those eighty damn fool animals keep right on eating. And you come here to—to——'

Harry said gently, 'If I were you, I'd sell them to some lunatic like me before he came to his senses.'


## CHAPTER SEVENTEEN

Fiero, the trader, rode up to El Paso and returned to the cantina about noon. His man Hilario came from the sleeping room Canty and Lute Harper were occupying and sat at the table with Fiero. The trader rocked his chair back and cleaned his nails with a knife.

'How are our guests?' he asked the old man.

'The feverish one is better, the well one is feverish. He bites at himself like a wounded animal. He paces the room without moving from his chair.'

'I wonder if the yellow one will shoot him?' Fiero yawned.

'*Quién sabe?* He would like to,' Hilario said.

'Since we sat on him while the doctor of horses opened his wound, he should thank us,' said the trader. 'But he won't. He's an ugly one.'

'The black one is uglier,' contended Hilario.

'At least he's got a little *cultura*. When I took him a cigar he said, "Thanks."'

'He's trying to get something out of you,' Hilario warned.

'Sure, but the other is *puro animal*. I wonder how long it will go on?'

'What about Don Harry?' asked the *muletero*. 'Did he leave on that stage today?'

Fiero snorted. 'There was no stage. The cow-eater of a commandant ran away and they have no escort. Damn their war, what are the rest of us going to do? Men are weeping for supplies in Sante Fe—but we're stuck here because of this foolishness.'

'No stage,' said Hilario.

'Don Harry was talking to me in the plaza. He wants to hire me for a guide.'

'A guide! Where to—to hell?'

155

'In the end, probably. He wants to get some stagecoaches together, sell tickets, and go to California. But he never will.'

'California . . . I have grandchildren in California. With plenty of men it should be possible.'

'It's *not* possible,' sighed Fiero, 'because his girl doesn't want to go. A beautiful woman. Hair like gold. But not one word did she say about California. She asked me if there was a good trail to Missouri.'

'A man is boss, is he not?'

'Only in the little things. You should know that, a man with grandchildren.'

Hilario linked his hands on the table. 'Yes. That's the way he's boss. But maybe Don Harry is different.'

'A man who would follow a girl twelve hundred miles, and fight a man in the river for her? Wake up.'

\*        \*        \*

Above Canty's head was a hole in the ceiling of willow rods and mud where mice came and went, starting small avalanches of earth each time they did so. On his ankle there was a sore spot because he could not keep his manacled leg still. He had the kind of big, muscular limbs which require exercise, and inactivity added to his wildness.

Every time he looked up, Lute Harper was

staring at him. Lute would smile at Canty then, and nod. And keep on staring, his eyes feverish and crazy. With that shining golden beard, he looked profanely apostolic.

'I got it figgered out,' Lute said suddenly.

'How you're going to kill me and get away with it?'

'How'd you know?' Luther carefully moved the injured leg.

'What else could you figure out, being you can only think of one thing at a time? Go ahead. How's it going to work?'

Lute rubbed the smooth stock of the rifle. It was a revolving Colt rifle with a side-hammer. 'I'm going to kill you at four o'clock day after tomorrow morning.'

'Can you wait that long?'

'Hell, I got to wait that long. Can't travel any quicker. At four o'clock, everybody's asleep. I blow your belly out and take off. In five minutes I'm across the river.'

Canty, rocking back in the chair, nodded sombrely.

'Pretty good, Lute. Then where do you go?'

On the floor beside the bed was a bottle of murky water. Lute took a long pull at it, spat out half a mouthful, and absently squinted down the barrel at Canty. Canty's belly sucked in and he almost groaned.

'Don't matter,' said Lute. 'Wherever I go, I'll have lots of time.'

'But no money.'

Luther grinned. 'No money, eh?'

'Not counting out-of-state currency. Did you bring it along?'

'Who knows?'

A quivering set up in the detective. 'Where'd you hide it?'

'Don't ask so many questions. I get all nerved up.'

'Then I'll tell you something,' said Canty hurriedly. 'I could make you the best trade a thief ever got: Good money for bad.'

'Now, how would you go about doin' that, Mr. Canty?' Lute was perfectly aware that Canty was arguing for his life, but he seemed almost naïvely to enjoy the performance.

'There's an old party in the stage depot that's got more double eagles than you got whiskers. I've been bunking with him. I wish I had his money, and he had a wart on his nose. One day when he was out, I checked through his luggage. There's a false bottom in one of his valises. I wish you could see what *I* saw.'

Lute's tongue showed between his lips. 'What'd you see?' A tiny crack had opened in his scepticism, and Canty set the wedge into it.

'It sounds so damn—so crazy,' he said. 'A man feels like a fool mentioning it.'

'Yeah? What?'

The strange part was that it was true. And that was why it was hard to tell. Something less fantastic, but completely false, would be easier to peddle. 'Did you read that time schedule

the stage company gave you with your ticket?'
Canty asked Lute.

'Can't read.'

'Well, they tell you not to carry any valuables on the stage. They don't want bandits holding up all their stages. But a big man like this Laymon Russell feels the same way about a fifty-dollar gold bar as we do about a two-bit piece. And yet enough gold to pay all his expenses for six months hefts like an anvil. Maybe he could cash cheques in California. Maybe not. So what could he carry to make sure he didn't have to work his way home?'

Lute's round-eyed attention was that of a child—an evil, dangerous child who liked stories about money and death.

'Diamonds,' said Canty. 'Rubies and diamonds.'

'Aw, now, listen—' said Lute, waking up crossly.

Canty struck the bedpost with the ham of his hand. 'Honest to God, Lute. It just figures. Jewels are good anywhere there's money. Where there's money and women, there's men buying jewellery. And in San Francisco there ain't anything but money and women. So Russell carries gems. Easy to hide, see? And light.'

Still the sleepy amber gaze scoffed. 'That there's a crock of baby mush,' Lute said.

'As God is my witness, Lute. And you could

have it all!'

'Why not you?'

'Because I'm not a thief. All I want is those banknotes to take home and buy my job back.'

'That's all you want, eh?'

Canty leaned back. 'No. I want your sister, too. To take back with me. And a fella named Logan.'

'How're we going to do all this?'

Canty rubbed a stiffness out of his neck. 'You can't travel yet, eh?'

'Maybe three–four days yet.'

'Can't hold up a stage when you start three days late. Maybe if you let me go, I could get the girl and valise and square with Logan—'

Lute wriggled down into the bedclothes. 'Git comfortable, Canty. You ain't leaving this room any way but dead.'

'That's your hard luck as much as mine. Because I could clean your record better than soap and water. I'll force a statement out of the girl that she and Logan and the others pulled the robbery . . . Or say I report you dead! I could say that I killed you in El Paso. Then you're off the record for good.'

Lute grunted. 'Ain't you got anything but lies in that big mouth? I'll tell you how I know you're lying about the jewels. If you'd'a found any, you'd'a kept them. That's just natural. So make yourself comfortable, friend. Keep tellin' me them good yarns and maybe I'll let you live till you run dry.'

'Well—as a matter of fact—' Canty began.

Lute's manner sharpened. 'Yeah?'

Canty shrugged. 'Never mind. Got some thinking to do.' He slumped down and scowled at his folded hands.

He had more than thinking to do before he discussed this with Lute again. There was some very careful work ahead of him, something in the nature of lapidary work.

An hour later, Paco, the barkeeper, came in with some food. He mentioned what he had heard from Fiero. The stagecoach to Indianola had been cancelled. Canty's head swam with optimism, joy, rage and despair. *If I have to cut my leg off to get out of here*, he told himself, *I'll do it.*

## CHAPTER EIGHTEEN

After he had talked with Fiero, Harry circulated among the saloons and rooming places and talked to potential passengers. They broke into two groups: Those who must get to California, and those who must travel east. The westbound adventurers wanted to leave not later than tomorrow. The eastbounders, scampering for home, talked about leaving before dark today.

'It's just an idea,' Harry told each. 'All that's sure is that it'll be westbound. I'm usually around the stage station if you want to see me.'

He went back to the stage yard and looked at the line of green and yellow coaches ranked along one wall. He passed behind the box stalls and inspected some of the stock. First-class; ready to roll—the whole kit-and-boiling. Now it was dark and he knew that Kelsey and Judith would have gone to dinner with Laymon Russell. He smelled food, and traced it to a corner near the main gate, where, behind his little canvas-curtained wagon, Allen T. Bird had a small pot of stew cooking.

'Pull up a rock,' Bird said. 'I hear you're going to California.'

'Where'd you hear that?' Harry squatted across the fire.

'In the plaza.' Bird fished some leaves from his pocket and crumbled them into the stew. 'That'll grow hair on your ears, boy. Kind you'll need to get to California. When do you leave?'

'When did the rumour say I leave?'

'Seven-thirty tonight. You're a half hour late already.'

'What I'm shooting for is not later than day after tomorrow. Can you cipher, Allen?'

'What's your problem?' Bird's blue eyes swam behind spectacles as thick as the bottoms of wine bottles.

'If I bought eight coaches at three hundred dollars apiece, how much would that be? Two thousand something?'

'Twenty-four hundred. You ought to have six mules to a coach and a dozen extra. Don't expect better than a hundred a head.'

'How much would that run?'

Bird figured some more, totalled, and it seemed Harry would need eight thousand four hundred dollars to make it. Harry grunted and sat back. 'Cash,' he muttered.

'Sell your tickets for cash.'

'Sure, but how much am I going to have to charge?' He had a rasping sense of irritation that he had to lean on someone for such simple work.

'Say ten passengers to a coach,' Bird began.

'Eight,' Harry corrected. 'I can't chance overloading. Each passenger I have is going to need attention. Decent food, blankets, medicine if I can find any in town.'

At a hundred and fifty a head, Bird reckoned, Harry could make it and have a little left over. 'What about salaries?' he asked. 'And grub to feed your men? Passengers will pay for meals like on any line, but the men have got to be fed. And horseshoes, spare parts and so on . . . This ain't the town to find bargains in, Harry.'

'That's where my money and my partners come in.'

The veterinary, taking a small desert flower from the brim of his hat, thoughtfully crumbled it into the pot. 'I'm going to need a doctor and vet, Allen,' said Harry.

Bird pursed his lips as he stirred the stew. 'I'm already spoken for,' he said.

'What do you mean? The Oxbow? I wouldn't give much for your chances of employment here.'

'Another feller is making up a train,' said Bird. 'Only he's goin' east. Ain't that surprising?'

'Laymon Russell?' asked Harry.

'Mr. Russell. But don't worry, son, I wouldn't travel across the street with Russell. I wanted to check his head bumps before I said yea or nay, but he wouldn't let me touch him. I say the man's got something to hide. Why else would a man act thataway?'

Afterwards Harry went to Kelsey's room. So Russell had lurked outside Woodsun's office and stolen his idea, he thought resentfully. With Russell's money, he could outbid Harry at every point. Harry tapped on the door.

'How about some exercise?'

Kelsey came out, pretty, blonde, cool-eyed in a pale blue cotton gown. She seemed more relaxed than since the Indianola stage was cancelled. They walked up the side street. 'Harry, the most wonderful news,' Kelsey said suddenly. 'Mr. Russell has a train ready to leave for Missouri.'

'I've got better news. Mr. Logan's train will leave for California in forty-eight hours.'

Kelsey looked away. 'No. I'm going back home. Last night, when I had to wait hours to

164

learn whether you were alive or dead, I knew I wasn't going to run any longer. I'm just not made for a fugitive.'

'If we go back, you'll go to jail, and Canty will stick that killing of Lute's on me.'

'We'll tell the truth. They'll have to believe us. I won't believe that innocent people go to jail.'

It was a nice thing for ladies to believe until they got into a jam, Harry decided; but it was no motto for a girl in trouble to stitch on her flag. 'Nobody *has* to believe us,' he stated. 'But they'll believe what Canty told 'em. What if that bank's already gone broke? Somebody's got to pay for it. That's the way it works.'

'I'll bet you've forgotten,' Kelsey said, 'that stages cost money.'

'I've even got ideas about money,' he said largely, 'I've got some, the tickets will bring in some, and I've got credit lined up for the rest.'

'Already?' she asked. She wore an expression that was not exactly a smile. So he knew she had guessed or anticipated it.

'I know how you feel about Judith,' he began, 'and I feel pretty much the same. Only of course—'

'I'm listening, Harry. Do go on.'

'She helped save my life,' Harry protested. 'I asked her what she meant by telling you I was dead. The best I remember, now she said she was trying to do me a favour. Anyway,' he swerved boldly, 'she—'

'No, no, go on about the favour,' Kelsey encouraged. 'I'm really interested, Harry.'

He tried to take her hands but she put them behind her. Harry protested. 'Is this what I trailed you across the country for?'

'I just have the feeling you trailed the wrong girl. When she was right beside you all the way. She must have felt pretty sure of you, to try to shoo me off like that.'

'Now do you see what I mean about trials? People will believe what they want to. I didn't say she was right—I just said I'm kind of in a corner. Because she did help save my life and my cash, so I owe her something.'

Kelsey's eyes filled suddenly. 'I'm mean and jealous, Harry,' she cried. 'But I do know I've got to go back, and try to clean it up.'

They walked back. They said goodnight and her door closed. Harry turned and saw Russell standing in his doorway.

'You can forget about your stage train, Logan. I've just talked to Woodsun again. He won't sell ten cents' worth of company property. We're stuck here.'

'We're stuck if we pull against each other.'

'We're stuck anyway. If you see Judith,' Russell added, 'send her back. She must have left while I was talking to Woodsun.'

Harry settled himself wearily on his pallet in a grain shed. Ideas kept bubbling up through his mind until sleep finally took over.

He was awakened by a voice yelling in

166

Spanish. Staggering with sleep, he groped to the yard. From one of the coaches lining the wall, flames rose bright and ragged as maple leaves. A workman was throwing handfuls of dirt at it.

The bucket brigade started at the well in the corner of the big fire-lit yard. Horses were squealing and kicking in the stalls. Harry and two other men rolled the stage away from the coach next to it. On the door panel of the second coach an oil painting already was blistered and smoking. Water from the buckets splashed against the burning stage as futilely as saliva. The thin poplar panels crackled like paper, the reach-and-bolsters settled down with steady oaken persistence to burn quietly to no ash at all. The axles succumbed first; the wheels tilted inwards; then the deck caved in with an Independence Day shower of sparks.

Harry was aware of Superintendent Woodsun moving at top speed; striding towards the grain shed for buckets, then checking himself to get a tarp with which to cover the nearest coach, but halting this project to seize the tongue of the burning stage and draw it farther from the wall. He never stopped shouting. In a few minutes it was over: A thousand dollars' worth of Abbott & Downing stagecoach was gone. If stagecoaches had souls, the spirit of this one was rising silently in the smoke of fine woods, leather, oil paint, and canvas.

Harry walked to the nearest stage in line to inspect the damage to it. There was some charring on the spokes and side panels, but that was all. As he turned he saw what looked like a small wedge lying on the ground. He was about to pick it up when Woodsun came charging towards him. Harry set himself, but the superintendent halted as if on leash, his features straining.

'What are you doing here?' Woodsun yelled, his Irish face working with muscular fury.

'I was fire-fighting,' Harry told him. 'I was asleep in the grain shed when it started.'

'But you were fire-*fighting,* not fire-*setting,* eh?'

'That's the truth,' Harry said.

Woodsun came close and peered into his eyes. 'Mister,' he said, 'I'm going to find out who set that fire. And by God and all the angels, if I don't kill him when I do—'

He wheeled and levelled his arm at a hostler. 'You! Stand guard the rest of the night. Sit up on that coach yonder and don't leave for five minutes. I'll sleep in the office.'

After the superintendent left the yard, Harry bent to pick up the object he had seen on the ground. It was the heel of a woman's shoe, the kind they called a Balmoral heel, and was covered with grey satin.

'Have you seen my daughter?' Russell had asked him.

*No*, Harry thought numbly, but *I think I*

168

*must have just missed her . . .*

## CHAPTER NINETEEN

He had meant to be up early to try to anticipate any further moves of Russell's. But when he opened his eyes, bright splinters of sunlight ran the length of the door and he could hear a persistent knocking. In wooden dullness, he sat up.

'Harry, wake up.'

Harry scrubbed his face. 'What's the matter?'

'Open the door.' It was Judith's voice.

He reached for his shirt. He went to the door, unlatched it and looked out. In the clear morning sunlight, the girl's black hair glistened like patent leather as she stood close to the wall. Her eyes were excited.

'Hurry,' she urged. 'He's with Woodsun right now!'

'Who's with Woodsun?' Harry brushed straw from his undershirt and began pulling his shirt on.

'My father-in-law. He's trying to beat us out.'

'Wait in the patio,' Harry growled.

He met her there, disciplining his hair with a steel comb as he came through the gate, his face still wet from the pump. An old Mexican was swishing the tiles of the courtyard with a wet mop. Judith sat on a bench near the *zaguán*, trying to appear composed. Harry sat by her, but she rose immediately. He pulled her down.

'Sit down a minute.'

'Don't you understand?' she said. 'He's already talking to Woodsun about buying the stages. But he wants to take them east.'

Harry laid something in her lap. 'I'm trying to find out who lost a heel in the stage yard last night.'

Judith sighed. 'Thank heaven! I knew when I lost it, but I couldn't stop. The watchman was coming around.'

Harry was astonished. 'You admit you did it, though? No alibi, even?'

She shrugged. 'I was just afraid you wouldn't think of burning a stage yourself. So I did it.'

Harry wagged his head. 'And the only thing to consider was getting caught. Judith, you just don't go around burning stagecoaches.'

'Harry, dear,' sighed the girl, 'it was perfectly plain that Woodsun would never sell them unless he was scared into it. Isn't that so?'

'All right! But it was wrong even if your reasons were right.'

Judith sniffed. 'I suppose you think you can get rich, like Father Russell, by turning the other cheek. Why, people like him are on the watch for turned cheeks. When they see one they hit it. It's the way business is done.'

'It's not the way I do business.'

'Do you want to get to the coast, or not?' asked Judith. 'Besides, in the long run the stage company will be ahead. If Woodsun doesn't sell, the coaches will be taken over by the Rebels. I just pricked the boil before it became a carbuncle.'

She rose grandly and gazed at him with irritation which turned to a chiding affection. 'Now, come on, Harry. We've got to make our offer before he signs up.'

'As a by-product of your bonfire,' he told her wryly, 'I can't show my face in his office now. He thinks I did it.'

'Well—it doesn't matter,' she decided. 'I can handle him. Just so I know you'll back me up, how much shall I offer him?'

Harry rubbed his ear. He was still rankling over what she had done, but by not going ahead now, he was putting his head on the block to wait for the axe.

'Start at two-fifty,' he said finally. 'Offer him seventy-five for the mules.'

\*       \*       \*

'It'd have to be all cash,' Woodsun was insisting. 'God knows I'm going out on a limb anyway. If I hadn't had that little seizure this morning I wouldn't consider—But it'd have to be all cash,' he repeated. 'I can't take any of your damned paste diamonds.'

Judith heard that much as she entered the long, cold office. The little fireplaces scooped into the walls at either end of the room did nothing to cut the autumn chill. She heard her father-in-law protest:

'Paste! I've got affidavits from the biggest jewellers in New York City—Hearing Judith, then, Russell looked around.

'Am I interrupting?' she said pertly.

'What is it?' Woodsun asked. He looked so pasty, so driven, that she pitied him. He had the blind, stony gaze of a statue.

'Mr. Woodsun and I are talking business,' snapped Russell.

'Oh, Father, you're not trying to sell those old—' She bit her lip. 'Oh, I'm so sorry . . .'

Woodsun leaned back in his chair, staring into the craggy face of the New Yorker. 'Is this how you finance your travels, my friend?'

Judith spoke quickly. 'Oh, I didn't mean they weren't perfectly good jewellery, Mr. Woodsun. I just don't care for those old-fashioned cuts. Mr. Woodsun,' she asked diffidently, 'is there any chance—well, it seems foolish even to suggest it. But I want to buy some stagecoaches.'

Woodsun laughed. 'Well, that makes three.'

'But I'm talking about real money—to be piled on your counter within the hour.'

Woodsun frowned and began to rock in his

172

chair.

'The price I thought of was two hundred and fifty dollars—' Judith went on.

'You've got no money!' shouted Russell suddenly.

'You *thought* I had no money.' Judith smiled. 'You thought you'd haul me to San Francisco and leave me there, didn't you? Or make me sign some sort of paper abandoning claim to your son's estate. So just to be safe, I brought what I could and sent some more by ship. You were born too late, Father Russell,' she told him. 'You should have sailed with Captain Kidd.'

\*       \*       \*

'*Today!*' the Mexican trader, Fiero, exclaimed. 'Why not tomorrow? Next week?' In the cantina, he was playing cards with Hilario and two other men. His sleeves were rolled up and his forearms were woolly with hair.

Harry had spent an hour signing up passengers and collecting down payments. '*Start packing,*' he had told them. '*If we leave, it'll be soon.*' He had made sure of Allen Bird and a mechanic; had signed up a wheelwright and two cooks. Then he had borrowed a horse and ridden across the river to try to secure Fiero as a guide.

'Tomorrow may be too late,' he said. 'If we only make a mile, I want to leave this afternoon.'

Fiero scowled. He played a card and shook his head. 'It would be the same all the way, "Hurry up! *Aprisa!*" '

Behind the bar, Paco, the bartender, was rolling dice by himself. 'You won't get far,' he said comfortably.

'Why not?' Harry asked him.

'Indians and *bandidos*. California!' Paco snorted. 'You won't get to Albuquerque.'

'Shut up,' suggested Fiero. 'Are you going to fight the Mexican War all your life? You'll have to make allowances for him,' he explained to Harry. 'His father distinguished himself at Chapultepec. He made a fortune stealing jewellery off the dead.'

Paco stiffly put the dice away and moved to the other end of the bar.

'What road will you take?' Fiero asked Harry.

'The mail road to Albuquerque. From there we'd take Beale's wagon road, unless you know a better one.'

'There is no better one,' said the old man, Hilario. 'Mountains, but easy mountains; Indians, but easy Indians—Navajos. Nothing hard till you cross the Colorado River. And by then the desert weather is perfect. Do you need a man who knows mules as a father knows his children?'

Fiero looked up. 'Are you quitting me?'

'No, *amigo,* I am going with you. You should

174

have some Mexicans for the camp work,' he counselled Harry. *'Muy listos* and they eat so little.'

'All right. Bring five or six of them with you. Three o clock?' he asked Fiero.

Fiero leaned back and scrutinized the ceiling for a time. 'California is a long way to go to see somebody else's grandchildren,' he sighed. 'All right! Three o'clock in the stage yard.'

*     *     *

Judith was waiting on the gallery of the depot. Crossing her arms, she said angrily, *'Dear* Father Russell!'

'What happened?'

'Both of us had our money here in time, but I couldn't win Woodsun over. He's selling each of us five coaches, and keeping two, in case. I have the bills of sale in my room. Only five.'

'What's Russell using for a crew?' Harry asked.

Secretly, Harry was relieved that he would have fewer passengers to worry about. Five coaches would still give him a working stable in California.

'Did you get our guide?' Judith asked.

'He's on the way. He'll bring his own mule-boss and some workmen. Any passengers show up yet?'

Judith laughed. 'A few of them are waiting

175

for you in the courtyard.'

Harry's mind was on Kelsey. Now that she had a choice of stages he was afraid she would pick Russell's. With her noble beliefs about juries and justice, she would hurry back to Missouri to tell her story and go to jail. But not if he could help it.

A clamour of conversation struck him as he entered the courtyard. He looked over the crowd and thought of a bivouac of soldiers. Sitting on carpet-bags and hand-trunks, or milling about, were forty or fifty men and a small seasoning of ladies.

The noise had a surge and ebb like an ocean. On hands and knees, before a map, one man was demonstrating something to another about the trails. In one corner of the courtyard a cluster of men was gathered about Laymon Russell. At that moment a man saw Harry and raised his arm to attract his attention. 'Mr. Logan!'

In a moment Harry was enclosed in a ring of excited travellers. Hands were on his sleeves, and everyone was trying to catch his eye. The voices were a barnyard gabble in his ears.

'Just heard about it, sir, and I—'

'If I can't get her to San Francisco, Mr. Logan, I don't know what will happen—'

'Never told us about this when we left, and—'

'Mr. Logan, my name's Harshaw, and I'm with the consular service—'

176

After they quieted a little, Harry announced, 'It will be three hours before we leave, folks. You might as well get some exercise or hunt up things you'll need on the way. Now, we've got an experienced Santa Fe trader to guide us. We'll have professional cooks and the best food I can find—which may not be much. But if we're to leave at all, I'll need the next couple of hours to myself. The passenger list is full, but there may be cancellations. Be in the street outside the gate with your baggage if you're wanting to get on.'

He went to Kelsey's room and knocked. The door opened at once. Her sleeves rolled, she was packing a suitcase which lay on one of the cots which now nearly filled the floor. She smiled absent-mindedly. 'Oh—come in, Harry.' She turned and went to the bed and standing with her back to him debated which of two garments to take. 'I like the flowered sacque,' she said, 'but the plain one is more practical. Still, it's not practical to take something you don't really favour, is it? But—'

Harry's hands compressed her waist and he kissed the back of her neck. Kelsey shivered. 'Does a stage operator have time for things like that?'

'A good stage operator is always on the alert for business. And you look like a prospect for a trip to California.'

'Perhaps, eventually . . . But it's Missouri, this trip.'

177

'Russell's no stage man,' Harry exploded. 'He'll never even get you to Kansas.'

'Why not? He's hired Butterfield employees for the trip. We'll go to Albuquerque and take the Cimarron short-cut.'

'Whatever trail you take, it will end in the same place, jail. In a few years, if you go with me, the charges will have to be dropped.'

'But there's no statute of limitations on disgrace. It would be fine for our children to be made fun of because there was a warrant for their mother in Missouri!'

Harry turned to the window. It was incredible that two people looking through the same window, could see such different views. 'I'm going to talk to Russell,' he said. 'He's got as much right to be heading up a wagon train as I'd have giving dancing lessons. But we might as well travel together to Albuquerque and make sure he gets that far.'

'That would be fine,' Kelsey said.

In the stage yard, Harry paused to speak to Russell. Before an audience of eager ticket holders, Russell was floating extravagant estimates of the speed his coaches would make on the trail, 'If those stages ever slow down for a minute.'

Harry interrupted, 'I'd like to see you in the yard.'

Russell followed soon, hands in pockets, a cigar in his mouth. Harry was lashing a cover over a wagon. He dropped the rope and confronted him. 'How far do you think you'll get with that outfit of yours? If you thought you saw some tough country in Texas, you'll die twice a day in New Mexico.'

'I know what kind of country it will be. But I'm prepared for it.'

'Then you'd better be prepared to swim the Canadian and the Arkansas, because there're no ferries.'

Russell's eye was cold and confident. 'Another approach to this would be for you to worry about your train and let me worry about mine.'

'It's going to take some experienced worrying to get you to Missouri, Mr. Russell. I'd be glad to help you worry until our trails split. Shall we throw in together for Albuquerque?'

Russell drew on the cigar. 'If it suits you. When can you leave?'

'By three or four.'

'All right. I'm ready now, but I'll wait.'

Harry's jaw clamped. 'I'd hate to hold you up,' he said. 'I'll tell my men to hurry.'


## CHAPTER TWENTY

'Good money for bad, boy—good money for bad,' Canty repeated. Lute was walking up and down the room, exercising his leg. It had been three days since Paco had come and said, 'Well, they're gone. Gone like yesterday, *señores.*' In Canty's head a wildness like the beating of wings was increasing.

Lute tried the leg, putting all his weight on it. 'Purty decent sawbones, that feller,' he muttered, glancing with wicked mirth at Canty. Then he said, 'Reckon I'll be travelling about daybreak tomorrow. Can you wait? Hell fire, if you ain't a purty sight, man.' He grinned. 'That's a trouble with some fellers—they git a steady job like yours and they just plumb let down. You ain't shaved in a week, Canty. You ain't hardly ate. You look awful.'

Canty knew how a caged tiger felt. Pacing to one end of the cage. Swinging his head to look out. Pacing to the other end. Swinging his head and peering out with yellow-eyed rage again.

'Good money for bad,' said Canty. 'I never thought I'd have to get a man to take diamonds and double eagles off me, Lute.'

Liking the ring of it, Lute echoed, 'Diamon's and double eagles. Man, that sounds purty. Diamon's and double eagles. But I got to pony up bullets and blood if I miss, don't I?'

It was Canty's first indication that Lute had considered the proposition at all. He choked on hope.

'Lute, ain't you got any faith in yourself? Don't you just know you can scare off a few mules in the dark and rap an old party over the head?'

'How's 'at work, now?' scoffed Lute. He had picked up his carbine and was working the hammer back and forth to see the cylinder turn.

'Why, hell, Lute'—Canty had to curb himself to keep from babbling—'what's the most important thing they're taking with them? Mules. If they lost them, they'd be cooked, wouldn't they? Now, listen to me. They're going to have to take some chances with those mules. At night they'll have to graze 'em. Maybe staked out; maybe just bunched under a few guards. Guards? Greasers! Ain't you as good as a greaser?'

Lute wiped his long nose with a finger. 'I say I am. I say I'm a shade better.'

'I say we both are,' affirmed Canty. 'All right, we're north of El Paso some place and we've chased their stock off. They've got a couple of boys on horses looking after 'em but it ain't any trouble to scare them off. Then we loop around to Russell's coach.'

'How do we know which is Russell's?'

Canty slowly began to smile. 'That's where I come in: I know him. I'm the one that can spot him.'

Now Lute grinned in turn. 'And that's where you go out, Mr. Canty. Because there ain't any jewels, and you damn well know it.'

'Look here,' Canty said. He pulled a hunting-case watch from his pocket. Lute came near but stayed out of reach. Canty opened the case carefully after inverting the watch so that the cover acted like a shallow pan; on its polished surface lay several small diamonds and rubies. Grinning, Canty looked up. 'No jewels, eh?'

Lute grunted. 'Them real?'

'You bet they're real. Ask Paco or somebody. Have 'em tested.' They were definitely real. Canty had, in his time, taken several pieces of jewellery off prisoners. The watch was one; a fob for a lodge to which he did not belong was another; a ring he wore was another. One by one, he had pried the small, cheap stones from these pieces since his last talk with Lute. He had turned the empty claws of the ring inside his palm.

'Be damned!' muttered Lute. 'Why didn't you show me the stuff before?'

'You were feverish,' said Canty plainly. 'I didn't know how you'd take it. I wanted you in your right mind before I got down to business. I reckon this settles whether I saw any jewellery or not, don't it? You'll be the simplest minded galoot that ever came out of Missouri, if you pass up this chance.'

'Two against forty,' growled Luther.

'And about thirty-five of the forty trying to catch stock! And some of the rest will be women.'

Lute's crafty mind was measuring carefully. 'So say we come off it all right: You think they ain't going to follow us?'

Canty rocked back in the chair, a long, hollow-cheeked black-stubbled man with dark fire in his eyes. 'That's what I think, Lute. I think Logan's going to stop a bullet this time. And you and I are going to be wearing greaser hats and those little blankets they call ponchos so nobody will know us.'

'Uh-huh,' Lute said. He was beginning to think more seriously about it.

'Now we've got you fixed up,' Canty went on swiftly. 'Let's slice *me* some cake, now: I want the girl. That'll be to your advantage, too. I'll haul her to Albuquerque with me and get on an eastbound freight string. She's going to take the load for all the Harpers except Fred, because I'm going to report you dead, and she won't know the difference.'

Lute's glance tipped up. 'But,' said Canty, 'if I don't get that currency back, the whole thing's off. And you don't have to worry that once I get the money I'll double-cross you and hit that stage myself. I'm not fool enough to think I can do it alone. And I imagine you'll be watching to make sure I don't try. Now where is that currency?'

Lute rocked back on his heels, grinning. 'Ain't much of a one for a fire in the evening, are you?'

'I don't get you.'

'If you'd built yourself a fire while you had my room in the depot, you'd have got smoked

183

out. There's three thousand dollars in notes in the flue, wrapped in an old newspaper. The rest's under the floor of that cabin Kelsey and I stayed in the night before we caught the stage.'

'I think we got a deal, Lute!' Canty's grin was a glint of white teeth in black stubble.

A man politely cleared his throat in the hall. Both men started as Paco came into the doorway. He wore a clean white shirt with puckered cuffs, was freshly shaven and his thinning hair was carefully brushed; by these tokens they knew he had been quite drunk the night before. Cleanliness was the tribute Paco paid his excesses.

'Well, well, well, gentlemen, are we planning a little trip?' said Paco heartily.

'You damned spy,' snapped Lute.

Paco shook his head. 'A spy is one who is not your friend. I am your friend. Else I could have had you killed days ago and saved the board money your friend left.'

A weary cynicism haunted Canty's eyes. 'You still could. What's the price not to?'

'No price. Oh, a favour perhaps . . . If you're going to Santa Fe you must have a guide. I can recommend a man named Jacinto. Very fine. He used to work for Fiero until he was fired.'

'Okay,' Canty said. 'What's Jacinto got to sell?'

'He would guide you until the train was sighted and then ride ahead and ask permission to accompany the train. But after a day or two he would decide to ride on and make better time. But he would come back instead, and tell you the things you need to know.'

'That would be a good man to have,' said Canty. 'How much?'

'Please yourselves,' shrugged Paco. 'When he was fired by Fiero they were in Indian country. Jacinto was captured and mistreated. Some call him Jacinto Tres Dedos—Three-fingered Jack. I think he would be pleased to help you.'

At least that was how Jacinto Tres Dedos was telling it, thought Canty sceptically. It was his observation that most Jacintos lost their fingers through digging into someone else's stew.

'You don't like this Fiero much, do you?' he said.

Paco pulled his mouth down. 'Fiero's all right. He's my cousin, and blood is thicker than water. But he thinks he's *gente decente*.'

'What's this henty-decenty?' asked Lute.

'"Fine people,"' translated Paco. 'Here it means, sometimes, a man who puts on airs. I believe you would like Jacinto. He would see you safely to Albuquerque or Santa Fe.'

'You don't miss much, brother,' said Canty wryly.

'I try not to, *patrón*, 'smiled Paco. 'You want him to find you some saddle horses and pack animals?'

Canty looked at Lute, who sucked a tooth. 'Sure.'

'How soon would you leave?'

Lute worked his stiff leg a bit. 'Oh—tonight, l reckon. No use gettin' bed sores around this trap, is there, Canty?'

'Not a damn bit, Lute. Want to unlock this leg iron now?'

Lute yawned. 'No hurry. We can still be friends, can't we?'

'If I wasn't already spoken for,' Canty said, 'I'd marry you in a minute.'

\*       \*       \*

They left Paso del Norte that afternoon. On the way, Canty paid a brief visit to the stage depot. The place was reasonably quiet, but the gallery and courtyard were still occupied by aimless, uneasy travellers talking of trails and guides, and home towns. Canty went to the room he had occupied before. He knocked, and a man in shirt sleeves, about fifty, with rumpled grey-brown hair, opened the door. He resembled a tough ranch foreman, and Canty was uncomfortable under his sharp gaze.

'Woodsun told me to check your fireplace,' he said. 'Has it been smoking?'

'Haven't had any firewood to find out.'

Canty brushed past him. 'It's just as good you didn't. The sweeps were working on it last summer and never got around to finishing. They left their roll of newspapers in the flue.'

He knelt on one knee and began clawing above the throat of the fireplace. The other man stood and watched Canty work. 'Man, you're going to wish you'd sent a Mexican to do that.'

Canty grinned, said nothing, and at that moment his knuckles struck a parcel of some kind and his nerves jumped as though triggered. He gripped the roll and pulled it out, and slowly stood up.

'So that's how they do it out here,' said the other.

'Yep,' said Canty. 'Excuse the trouble, mister. I'll have some firewood sent over.'

'Would you do that?'

Canty walked out and rejoined the two horsemen around the corner. He mounted, and he and the Mexican, Jacinto, each held the lead rope of a pack animal as they left town. They travelled ten miles that night, stopping at a deserted relay station called Frontera. Lute's leg was giving him some trouble. The guide, Jacinto, was a short, strong man with raisin-brown skin and a smooth, fat nose shaped like a parrot's beak. He spoke fair English. As they were building a fire to prepare some food, he announced, 'They stop here too.'

Lute peered into the darkness quickly. 'Who? Somebody comin'?'

'He means Logan's party stopped here,'

Canty said. 'How do you know, boy?'

'They make—*como se dice?*—tracks all around.'

'Yeah, I see 'em now,' Canty declared. 'How fast you think they'd travel?'

'Not very fast. No change of horses.'

Canty watched how the three fingers of his right hand held a machete to chop kindling. 'Well, we don't want to miss 'em, do we?'

Jacinto shook his head. 'We don't miss them.'

## CHAPTER TWENTY-ONE

The first four days were hard. The passengers did not adapt well to sleeping on the ground, and the ladies yearned for warm baths and fresh vegetables. Forty-three passengers and eighteen employees were Harry's worry, but Fiero handled all the workmen ably so that Harry had time to mother the passengers.

He noticed that they stayed in character. If a man worried about whether there were Indians in the brush along the river, he would worry also about whether the antelope shot yesterday was too green to eat or perhaps too gamy. A woman who wept over her children at home in Massachusetts would have the weak trembles over two men having a falling-out over what had sat outside in the dust longer.

But on the fifth day the screw began turning more easily into the wood. Suddenly everyone was used to sleeping on straw, and the ladies were accustomed to being dirty. Allen T. Bird spent only twenty minutes at sick-call that morning and by eight o'clock the slow caravan was rocking along the rough brush-fringed road on the east bank of the Rio Grande, the oldest highway on the continent. Riding beside his lead stage, with Judith inside it, Harry heard the black-birds fussing in the yellow cane-thickets beside the river and liked the sharp bare hills paralleling the road on the right. He was hopeful. Kelsey had not listened to any more of his arguments, but she watched more closely when he was talking to Judith. Fiero estimated four more days to Albuquerque.

And it was on that fifth day that a Mexican rider jogged in during the noon rest and politely asked for the boss-man. He came to where Harry and Judith were lunching in the shade of a stagecoach. The travellers ate in messes of seven. Standing there pressing his big sombrero against his belly, his free hand holding his horse, the man said, 'I call myself Jacinto Gallegos, *patrón*. I beg the favour to travel with your train.'

Harry looked him over. He was well set-up and had a nose like a small brown banana. He wore a folded red and grey serape over his shoulder. The thickness of his nose made his eyes seem close together. The eyes were very light, a brindle colour.

'Where you from?' Jacintor asked Harry. He sipped coffee and watched him.

'Paso del Norte, *patrón*. I have business in Santa Fe but I fear to travel alone.'

'You got this far, didn't you?' Harry wanted to hear him talk a little more before he made up his mind about him. Also he saw Fiero coming from where he had been fitting a mule with a rawhide shoe.

'Si, *patrón*. But it is more dangerous from here on. I would cook for you or whatever you wish.' He gave a smile as mirthless as a monkey's.

'Well, I don't know, Jacinto. What kind of business you got in Santa Fe?'

'Hides, *patrón*.'

'In business for yourself?'

Fiero came to stand a few feet from the Mexican, just looking at him. Jacinto saw him. Colour mounted into his throat and face. *'Hola! Qu'ubole?'* exclaimed Jacinto. 'Makes much time, my cousin, since—'

'You want to lose the other three fingers?' Fiero asked coldly.

Jacinto's smile faded and he said, 'Blood is thinner these days, Fiero, since you make money.'

'I make more money,' said Fiero, standing very close to him with his hands on his hips, his severe poker-features set, 'now that I do not

190

have you stealing from me.'

Jacinto fervently raised his hand. 'I say again, cousin, someone who hated me put the things in my saddlebag.'

*'Ándale!'* Fiero said. 'Travel by yourself. Where you ride, flies collect.'

Jacinto bowed his head. Glancing apologetically at Harry, he said, 'Well, *patrón*, may you pass a good journey.'

'Sorry,' Harry said.

From another group of diners, Laymon Russell's voice called brusquely. 'Come over here, will you?'

Jacinto touched his breast. 'I?'

Russell made a hand gesture and the Mexican led his horse over. Nearby, Kelsey watched with disapproval for Fiero. 'Do you know the trails?' asked Russell.

'What trails, *señor*?'

'The trails to the Mississippi River.'

Jacinto smiled uncertainly. 'I heard you were going to California.'

'Some of us are. Others are going east. I own the stages that are going east, and I'll need a man who knows the trails.'

Jacinto went to one knee and, vaquero fashion, laid his hat on the ground to think better. He made a line in the earth. 'From Albuquerque a good wagon road goes to the Canadian River and down it to Fort Smeet.'

'Smeet?' said Russell. 'Oh—Smith. What about a more northerly trail?'

Jacinto made another mark. 'The Cimarron short-cut is pretty good, *señor*. Or the Santa Fe trail by Bent's Fort.'

'When you get through talking,' said Fiero, 'get out of here.'

Russell's head raised. 'See here,' he rapped, 'if I hire him it will be my business, not yours.'

'Fine. But it will be between Jacinto and me if he doesn't get out.'

Russell's keen grey eyes travelled down Fiero's short, solid frame and back up to his squarish features. 'Nevertheless,' he said, 'he's hired. What are you going to do about that?'

'I'm going to kill him.' Fiero smiled at last, drawing and cocking his revolver.

Jacinto rose and gave Russell a sourish, what-do-you-expect-from-him smile, and swung into his saddle. 'Well, *adiós!*' he said cheerfully. As he rode away, Russell marched up to Fiero. 'I'd like one thing understood—'

Fiero said to Harry, 'I'll ride ahead and see that he keeps moving.' He turned his back on the older man and went to saddle.

'Isn't he perfect?' Judith said to Harry.

\*　　　\*　　　\*

That night, Jacinto told Canty and Luther, 'There is a blessing on thy endeavours, amigos.' He had ridden in at dark, five miles behind the Logan train, and was mixing water with his *atole* by their fire, in the shell of an

192

old ranch building. His smooth brown face was greasy with the sweat of pleasure.

Canty chewed jerked beef and watched Jacinto's eyes. He despised the man. *Maybe it's the sore on my ankle from that shackle*, he told himself. But he had reached the point where he almost hated himself. He felt like a grimy pawnbroker down a dirty alley, buying, with something stolen, something filthy but precious to him—treachery. When had it come to be precious? When he was born, probably. But only lately had it appeared filthy to him. He used to call it justice, but justice was snowy, and how come things as soiled as Lute Harper's craving for money, and Jacinto's lust for revenge, provide the materials for anything good?

'Okay, I'll ask it,' Lute sneered at Jacinto. 'What's new?'

Jacinto shaved cake coffee into a cup. Smiling, he announced, 'Thy friends part at Albuquerque. The blonde woman goes east with the old man with the head like a stone. My cousin and Logan travel east. The old man's crew will give thee little trouble.'

'What's this thee-thy talk?' snorted Canty. 'You a Mormon priest or something?'

Jacinto's face registered injury. 'In my language it is used among close friends. If I took a liberty—'

'You did. You and us are as close as we'll ever be right now. Well, that's good news about Russell and the gal. But it ain't going to get you a shot at your cousin, is it?'

Jacinto gazed at Lute. Lute was massaging his bad leg. 'Since Señor Lute goes west also, we will ride from the Russell train to my cousin's train, after you have what you want from the girl . . .'

*He's sticking it into me,* Canty thought, and he glanced sharply at him. 'I'm a lawman,' he said. 'What I want from the girl is her testimony against her brothers. What Lute wants is some of the junk that fool Russell's packing. Maybe he'll go shares with you. You wouldn't care if it had a little blood on it, would you?'

'Have some grub and shut up,' said Lute.

'That's good hardheaded advice,' admitted Canty in a moment. 'If everybody was as honest as you are, it'd put Colonel Colt out of business.'

Lute gave a little laugh. It was his kind of humour. Canty tasted his food, muttered, 'Slop,' and threw it on the ground. 'I'm hittin' the hay,' he said.

And as he lay there sleepless, his hatred of Harry Logan opened like a night flower, and he felt poisoned by the fragrance of it. Because, more than anyone else, Logan was responsible for turning to lead the gold of Pete Canty's currency.

# CHAPTER TWENTY-TWO

At Albuquerque, a town of dun adobe buildings on a dun-coloured plain, there were primitive stores and services. The cottonwoods along the river were golden, the sky was as bright as Indian jewellery, the air had the chill of white wine. They lay over one night at the Overland Mail depot. Service on the Santa Fe road was on a fortnightly basis. There were two hostlers on hand; and the mail agent, who ran a fed business, helped with final preparations of both trains. By noon, Harry had been ready to leave for three hours, but he made work so that the Russell party would leave first.

Russell had been gone for two hours, hunting a guide. Fiero and Hilario sought Harry among the coaches. 'We aren't getting to San Francisco very fast, *amigo*,' Fiero said drily.

'Fifteen minutes,' Harry said.

'What are we waiting for?'

'We're waiting because I want them to leave first. If we go first, it'll look like I walked out on her. I don't want that on my conscience.'

Fiero said, 'I said to Hilario in Paso del Norte that you'd never go to the coast, because your girl wouldn't go. Now I say it to you.'

'I say that at twelve-thirty we stretch out.'

Fiero took a coin from his pocket and handed it to Hilario. 'A gold dollar says the same thing I say.'

'You just lost a dollar,' Harry said, putting his coin in Hilario's hand.

'*A ver!*' scoffed Fiero.

When Russell returned to the stage yard, he was triumphantly in possession of Jacinto Gallegos. Fiero stared at them as they hurried to where the tarps were being lashed down over the supply wagons.

'That cow-eater,' he exclaimed. 'He's going to guide them after all!'

'Is he as bad as you say?' Harry asked.

'Figure it yourself: I gave him work because he was my cousin, though he knew nothing but dancing and tickling a girl's chin. In two weeks he was stealing from my cash-box.'

They heard Russell call, 'Will everyone go to his coach, please? We leave in five minutes.'

'Hitch 'em up,' Harry told Fiero. He went to where Kelsey and two other women sat in the cool sunlight on the stone ring of a well. Kelsey rose as she saw him coming. They walked to her coach. Harry stood beside her and held her hand in silence. At last he spoke, saying all he thought there was to say.

'I love you, Kelsey.'

She turned. 'Don't you love me enough to see me through this?'

'I love you too much to lead you to slaughter, honey.'

196

'Harry,' Kelsey whispered, 'I'd shave my head or live in China or take in washing if you wanted me to. But I'm made differently from you. I have to know what's in a room before I rush into it. I don't want to have to explain to my children that even though I'm a fugitive, I'm really innocent. Who could ever believe me?'

'Maybe nobody. But the apple-cart's been upset now, and we've got to save the apples we want most. What I want is to be on the outside, making my own way.'

'Then you'll have to do it that way. And I have to do it my way.'

Harry sighed. After a moment he said, 'That fellow Jacinto is no good. Fiero says he stole from him, and he doesn't even know the trails. Do you want to travel with an outfit like that?'

'Perhaps Fiero is no good.'

Harry threw up his hands. 'So be it! If we're going to fuss over everything, maybe we're doing the right thing after all.'

'I hope we are,' Kelsey said. 'Kiss me good-bye, Harry.'

'It's *hasta la vista*, not good-bye,' Harry said. Yet when he left her, it was more like a book closed than a page turned down.

\* \* \*

The broad, flat plain promised nothing but loneliness and wind. The road along which the

197

stages and high-sided supply wagons moved was mediocre. Before sundown they covered twelve miles, so that the desert city behind them was out of sight but the horizon promised nothing at all. A week of this could pass, Harry thought, and the travellers would have little feeling of accomplishment. In the journal of the trip he was keeping, he could not record *Passed Rabbit's Ears Peak*, or *Camped at Cedar Creek*, but simply, *Made 12 miles*. An ant touring the circumference of a hoop could make the same notation.

Fires were built, the stages and wagons ringed up, stocktenders drove out the mules, and the richness of frying meat spiced the air. Judith, Harry and Fiero ate dinner at the employees' mess.

Harry ate silently while they talked. 'What's the road like on that Cimarron short-cut?' he asked suddenly.

Judith leaned forward. 'Harry,' she said, 'we're going to California. Don't forget that, will you?' Her voice was sharp with irritation.

'We're travelling, aren't we?' Harry said. 'But the farrier was telling me the Indians get mighty bronco on that Cimarron road sometimes.'

'Like any of them,' shrugged Fiero.

'Fiero,' urged Judith, 'will you ask Mrs. Walker if she's feeling better now? She was ill this afternoon.'

Then she reached for Harry's hands, smiling

198

at him. 'Do you know what you remind me of? A man about to be married. You don't know whether you want to go ahead with it or not. But it's different, now. You're already married. Married to forty-some passengers and a business. And it's time you settled down.'

'I'm settled, all right,' Harry declared. 'I'm going to California, and there's no two ways about that.' *So why do I keep looking back over my shoulder?* he wondered.

'Because if you don't go to California,' Judith pursued, 'you lose all the money you put into our little venture, and all the coaches you'd share title to when we got there.'

'All right! But you can't blame me for worrying, can you? Your father-in-law will probably beach the whole train somewhere in New Mexico.'

'Probably,' Judith agreed. 'If it weren't for Kelsey, I'd say I *hope* so. But Laymon Russell runs to luck the way some people run to red hair. He might roll into Independence, Missouri, without so much as a fleck of mud on the coaches.'

Harry set down his tin plate and walked to the back of the coach. Standing there, he gazed across the greyish-pink plain under the clear, pale evening sky. Distantly he could see hills ribbed with shadow. A blur of smoke showed where Albuquerque lay across the river. The desert was quiet, cool and serene. But danger was often serene until it leaped from the brush like a cougar. Guided by a light-fingered wagon train renegade, the Russell party would probably never cross the Canadian. They were going unprepared into bronco Indian country, a country of little water and scarce game. There was no doubt that they were travelling towards tragedy. And Kelsey was going with them.

Harry turned, his decision made. He had been foolish to let her start at all. But it was not too late to follow and bring Kelsey back, tied hand and foot if necessary. Having decided it, he felt suddenly calm.

He walked to a supply wagon and began collecting things for the ride. Figuring they had travelled ten miles, he had an all-night ride ahead of him. He put food in a saddle-bag. Returning to the stage, he took his coat from inside it.

'What do you think you're doing, Harry?' Judith asked. She was standing near the stage with her arms crossed, watching with cool disapproval.

'I'm going to bring her back. I was crazy to let her start.'

'She won't come back, Harry, and you can't force her. She's not a child.'

'She is when it comes to horse sense.'

'You think you can make her travel a thousand miles with us? She'd never forgive you.'

'But I'd never forgive myself if I didn't go

after her.'

Judith came to him and slipped her arms about his neck. She peered gravely into his face, looking very desirable in the dusk, and rather sad. 'Are we just business partners after all, Harry?'

'That's the arrangement, isn't it?'

'I hoped it would grow into a better arrangement. Oh, Harry! Is it because I'm married? Because I won't be forever, you know. Even if Louis doesn't die . . .' She shuddered. 'That sounds terrible, but do you know what's even more terrible? Louis. He's weak, and silly, and he has a hundred lady friends and none of them cares for anything but his money. But now he's off playing soldier so he can come back with a scratch or two and strut like a banty rooster for them. But if he comes back, he'll strut without much money, because I've transferred most of it to a San Francisco bank. I hoped you and I could go so many wonderful places with that money.'

Harry realized there was a kinship between them, for they had both come up from nothing. They had fought with what weapons they had, and if his weapons were skill and stubbornness and industry, hers were beauty, cleverness and cold-bloodedness. It was a cat's instinct to be sly; but it was his instinct to distrust slyness. And something more than instinct was pulling him out of her arms now.

'It's pretty complicated,' he told her. 'I've got

this old-fashioned notion about not planning marriage with married women. And on top of that I have peculiar feelings about Kelsey. I don't know what to call them but love. I really thought what you and I were going into was business.'

Judith bit her lip as she looked at him, not hurt but annoyed. 'There's a neater way of saying all that, Harry: "Can't we be friends?"'

'Well, yes,' Harry agreed. 'Can't we?'

'Well, no! You can't be just friends with a girl who is in love with you. You've got to be either her lover or her enemy.'

'That's foolish.' Harry picked up his saddle and started for the line of horses cross-tied between two wagons. He heard her following.

'If you go, you needn't ever come back,' she warned.

'I have to come back. I work here.'

Catching his arm, she turned him, her face full of colour. 'Listen to me, Harry. I didn't back you just because I thought you'd make money for me. I want to marry you when I can. I suppose you think if I saw some other man I liked I'd do it all over again?'

Harry permitted himself to smile. Judith slapped him. 'How do you know you don't love me?' she asked. 'Men are always marrying girls just because they—they can't make love to them any other way. How do you know that isn't the trouble with you?'

'I just don't think it is, Judith, I like you.

You're a funny girl, but you're quite a woman.'

'Are you ever jealous of Kelsey?' Judith demanded.

'She's never given me cause to be.'

Judith smiled. Then she gave a strained little laugh. 'Well, I'm going to give you cause to be, if you leave me alone tonight.'

'What do you mean?'

'I'll go for a long walk with Fiero . . .'

Harry looked at her. He tied the horse again. Stepping into the clearing, he called, 'Fiero!'

'What's the matter?' the Mexican called through the dusk. He was sitting by the stagecoach, finishing his dinner. He stood up now, and sauntered across the ground.

'I've got to be gone tonight and most of tomorrow,' Harry told him. 'Miss Judith has a feeling she might be tempted to burn a stagecoach while I'm gone. Will you see that she doesn't?'

Fiero shrugged and looked at the girl. 'We ain't got enough trouble, so you're going to fetch us another girl, eh?'

'That's right. You know how it is. I won't be gone long.'

'You better not be, *compadre*. These people are going to be climbing my back wanting to head for California before you get back.'

'Tomorrow night sure,' said Harry.

# CHAPTER TWENTY-THREE

According to plan, Canty and Lute Harper left the river road and rode north-west after Jacinto left them. They were heading for a notch in the hills which he had described to them. They located the notch easily, a broad pass through some low, brushy hills. They rode up the toe of the hills at the south end of the pass, crossed over the crest out of sight from anyone approaching from Albuquerque, and made camp. Since they were many hours ahead of the Russell train, which was due to camp in the pass that evening, they chanced a fire and had a hot dinner. Canty looked suspiciously at Lute's ugly, wasted face as he gulped his food, and felt relieved.

*God bless your simple mind*, he thought. *When we raise Santa Fe, I'll have the nicest surprise for you.*

He had a warrant for Lute's arrest, but probably it wouldn't do much good. And if it did, he would be robbed of the blessed joy of squaring with Lute for those days in his stinking sick room looking down a rifle barrel. He thought deliciously of pouring the slugs into him like pebbles into a water-melon. He did not think of it as killing: It was more like exterminating.

After eating, they climbed back to the ridge,

from which they could see the desert. Later that day they saw the dust of a wagon train to the west, and before dark the stagecoaches were lined up at the foot of the long talus slope beneath them. Little fires blazed in the dusk, and three men rode out with the stock. Lute chuckled.

'Yonder goes ol' Jacinto with the stock. Last they'll see of *them* mules!'

In a half hour, the darkness pulling in snugly, they witnessed Jacinto's return from placing the stock. The stocktenders had instructions to keep right on going with them and sell them where they could, for what they could. The stage train was now stripped of horses and mules.

Canty sat on the ground with his back against a rock, watching. Nearby Lute was observing with brutish calm.

'You reckon that greaser's dependable?' he grunted.

'He'll do as he's been told. What he wants is Fiero. But Fiero isn't with this train, so if he's to get your help in following Logan and skinning out Fiero, he's got to do like he's told.'

'Old Russell in the rear coach, the gal in the next ahead, eh?'

'Uh-huh.' Canty got up. 'I'm going to have some more coffee. They'll all be asleep in an hour and we'll have the Mex's signal.'

But it seemed like several hours before they

heard a man whistling softly at the camp. Both men rose quickly from the ground on the ridge above the pass, where they had returned to wait. They picked up the folded ponchos on which they had been sitting, candy-striped Mexican blankets like short hall-rugs with a slot in the centre of each. 'Hell of a way to treat a good blanket,' said Lute, pulling the poncho over his head.

Disguised as much by the darkness as their costumes, they walked their horses down the hill, letting the animals pick their delicate way through the Spanish bayonet, brush and rock. A hundred feet from the camp, they halted and studied the lay of things. The coaches were arranged in a straight line just off the road, their tongues pointing out for easy access in the morning. Coals, and a single blazing branch were all that remained of the fire. The drivers and a few male passengers slept near the fire, and atop the coaches could be seen blanketed forms of sleeping passengers. A man in a conical Mexican sombrero squatted near the fire, smoking. Now he dropped the remains of a thin black cigar in the coals and walked silently to the rear of the line of coaches and waited there.

Canty tied his horse quickly to a stunted desert cedar and the two men joined Jacinto. 'The old man sleeps inside,' he said softly. 'The girl is in the coach ahead, but I do not think she sleeps. Better to take care of her first.'

'I think so,' said Canty. He had cords, a cloth for a gag. 'You kept a horse for her?'

Jacinto tilted his head. 'In the brush. I bring it.'

'Hurry up. We'll be ready when you get back.'

'Jacinto?' a girl's voice called softly.

The Mexican straightened like a soldier. *'Si, señorita!'*

'Is someone with you?'

'The stock-tenders, *señorita*. You should sleep.'

'Shouldn't they be with the stock?'

'The mules and horses are picketed. The men rode in for coffee. Now they go back.'

Canty jerked his thumb and Jacinto moved off. He paced quietly towards the coach. Faintly he could see the girl's head at a window. With Lute close behind, he reached the coach. Without hesitation, he reached inside through the window and slapped his hand over the girl's face. She now began to struggle and attempt to bite him, but he held a thick pad of cloth in his palm. Lute ripped the door open, and reaching into the stage he seized Kelsey's wrists. The plank bed was made up and she lay on it close to the door. In savage silence, they worked at tying her hands and feet and securing the gag over her face.

Then it was done, and Canty stepped back, panting. Lute was gasping for breath, his face gouged with deep shadows. Canty hated that face for the filthy enjoyment of the girl's terror.

'We picked your peach, boy! Now let's pick mine!' Lute said. 'Hey, here comes Jacinto.'

They strode back to Laymon Russell's coach, and here it was as simple as opening a door. The old man, lying on the planks, reared up with a grunt. 'What's the matter? What is it?'

Jacinto was just behind Canty, ready to help. Lute leaned in through a window. 'Ever'thing's just fine,' he murmured. He crashed the stone he had picked up solidly upon Russell's head. The old man sank back with a whistling of breath through his lips. Canty moved back, letting Lute do the searching. He and Jacinto carried the girl to the waiting horse, untied her feet and installed her in the saddle, after which Canty tied her ankles beneath the horse. Lute came running up with a valise.

'This it?' he panted.

Canty opened it, threw out clothing, found the catch at the bottom of it. He raised the false bottom and Lute almost shoved his head into the valise. 'Well,' he muttered, 'them's jewels, all right.'

Canty tasted the smell of him, his breath, his body—a stench like a rancid lynx. His stomach lurched towards his throat.

'Damn it, let's go,' he said.

They rode east on the wagon road, passing through the gap. Canty and Kelsey rode in the lead. The railroad man pulled up and looked back at Jacinto.

'Don't miss the short-cut. We're not going to Santa Fe by way of Fort Smith.'

'No, I won't miss,' said Jacinto with a strange, stiff smile.

'Me neither,' said Lute Harper. He pulled back the hammer of the revolver he had drawn. 'Don't reckon I could, at this range. Hey, Canty?'

There was the shock, the flash, the roar. Canty spurred his horse.

## CHAPTER TWENTY-FOUR

Around ten o'clock that night, Harry rode into Albuquerque. In all the town there was scarcely a light. Now and then he saw candlelight in a *jacal* as he passed. All the little low buildings about the plaza were closed and shuttered, but at the stage station there was a Mexican watchman. Harry made him understand that he wanted to talk to the mail agent. The agent came from the station tucking his nightshirt inside his trousers.

Harry made a trade with him: His horse and ten dollars for a spring wagon with a two-horse team for the night. Sometime tomorrow he would return with the wagon and make arrangements to be driven to the stage camp.

After he left town, he picked up the road trailing east towards some foothills. There was a frosty curl of moon drifting low over the hills, and he headed towards it while the horses scuffed along the ruts and night birds flicked past his ear, and coyotes yipped and snarled in chorus in a gully nearby.

The road crippled along like an old man on two canes, trailing south to ease around the toe of a desert mountain. The moon climbed until it was gazing down on him. Harry grew restless. There was something unsettling in being on an east-running trail at all, when his destiny and safety were in the west. Like a hawk on a limb, he sat hunched on the wagon seat, giving the horses a flick of the whip from time to time.

He felt he was overdue for the camp. Maybe Russell was more of a pusher than he had figured him for. He had expected to find the train half-stalled, half-camped much closer to town. Then he saw a fire burning in the darkness far ahead, and at once he knew that it was Russell's party. But why a fire at this time of night? It must be three or four o'clock, he reckoned.

He let the horses out. After a while he could see that the fire was at the base of a hill just south of the road. The horses flicked their ears forward and one of them whinnied. The blaze was too big for a warming-fire for wranglers, and Harry knew someone was sick or that something had gone wrong. As he drew closer he saw that the stages were not ringed up but had been left in line. Then he could make out, against the firelight, the forms of men coming and going.

As he left the road for the last hundred yards through the brush, he heard a sound like the Israelites at the wailing wall, and about the fire he could see men and women moving about. Harry stopped the wagon near the stages. A man lay on a blanket near the fire. Two men were looking down at him and a woman sat near him rocking and weeping loudly. Harry recognized the man. It was Russell.

As he walked towards the fire, he looked for Kelsey. He did not see her, nor did he see Jacinto, and he looked for someone he knew. When he reached the blanket, the woman looked up and recognized him.

'Oh, thank God, thank God, it's Mr. Logan . . .' Then she fainted.

One of the men knelt to help her. Harry went to one knee beside Russell. The man's face was bloody. He wore a nightshirt over long underwear, and his lips were moving as he stirred slightly on the blanket. Men and women were beginning to assemble, all trying to tell Harry what had happened. A man crouched by Harry. It was Taylor, one of the drivers.

'I knew something like this would happen,' he said. 'I told Mr. Russell that Mexican was no good. But he had his own ideas.'

Russell's eyes opened. They looked yellow and glazed. 'Get him some water,' Harry ordered. 'What happened?' he asked Taylor.

'Well, God'n I don't hardly know. See, this chucklehead hires a couple more men for wranglers in Albuquerque. Tonight he and them take the stock out to graze, and we settles down. Here, gimme that water,' he said to the man who had brought it. He held it to Russell's mouth. 'Then something woke me up and there was this kind of scuffling. I got up and yelled, 'What's goin' on?' Like that, 'What's goin' on?' but all I heard was somebody groanin'. When I got up, here was Mr. Russell out colder'n a well chain in January and a cut acrost his head.'

Russell drank a little, but most of the water ran from his lips. 'When was this?' asked Harry.

'Couldn't 'a' been forty minutes past.'

'Well, did you scout around any?'

'On what?' said someone. 'There ain't a horse in sight.'

Russell seemed to recognize Harry. He gazed at him fixedly and tried to speak. Only a sound like that of a sleeper moaning to himself came from his lips.

'You didn't see who clubbed him?'

'No.'

Harry asked the question he had delayed asking. 'Isn't Kelsey Harper up?'

'Well, God'n where *is* she?' said Taylor, staring around the fire. 'Anybody seen Kelsey? Well, now ain't that—'

Harry asked, 'Somebody take care of Russell. I want to look around. Which coach is hers?'

'Next to the back. Mr. Russell was sleeping alone inside the rear one. Mrs. Bailey, you were sleeping in the coach with Kelsey, weren't you?'

'No, sir,' a woman said, half weeping. 'That fellow Jacinto asked me to double up with Mrs. Strawn, because he was going to have to work on our coach before sunup.'

It was clear that he would find nothing, but Harry ran to the stage. The door on the far side, against the hill, was open. Inside, where the plank seats had been let-down, some rumpled blankets showed that the bed had been used. Some garments hung as curtains in the windows. Far off, a gun popped. Harry stood up straight. Again he heard a gunshot, and he turned his face up and stood perfectly still, listening.

He ran back to the fire. On the way he saw one of the saddles on the ground, and he carried it with a bridle to his wagon. He was saddling one of the horses when Taylor hurried up.

213

'Say, did you hear them shots?'

Harry tightened the girth and said, 'Get me a rifle. Hurry up.'

Taylor brought a rifle. 'That's a two-shot, Harry. There's a Colt rifle around too, but—'

Harry swung up. 'Never mind. You saddle that other horse and look for the stock. Saddle anything you can ride and follow me. Don't suppose they'll be far.'

'Okay. Say, Russell's talking now. It was *three* fellers, he says. And they were all dressed in ponchos and big hats, but he thinks one of 'em was named—was it Cantry?'

'That's close enough.'

*　　　*　　　*

It was too dark, despite the moon, to pick up a trail among all the tracks about the camp. Harry rode to the top of the little hill behind the stages and gazed about the desert. Out there somewhere Canty, his evil shadow having caught up with him for the last time, was moving rapidly away. Canty's glib tongue had cut through Lute's suspicions and made an ally out of him. Harry's hands made a frame about his eyes as he turned slowly, scanning the plain. But he could discern nothing farther than a few hundred yards away, except the faint trace of the road through the desert.

Would they stay on the road? Not knowing the country, they would almost have to. Which way would they head? He had not passed them coming out, so if they were on the road they were travelling east. Canty would head east anyway. But not Lute. And now, remembering the shots, it began to settle out in his mind: Canty had finished with Lute. He had settled accounts and was heading for home.

Harry rode down the hill to the road and loped north-east on it. Fiero had told him it ran to Las Vegas and split there into three routes to the east. He estimated the distance from which the shots had come. About a half mile out he stopped and got down to look for hoof prints. The moon was behind him and underscored with thin shadows every break in the earth. The road was little travelled these days, but it carried the prints of three or four horses. Canty, Kelsey, Lute and Jacinto. Everything added up except Lute's travelling east. Probably, for strength, they would hang together for a few miles. A little farther along he would find Lute, and then there would be three sets of hoof prints.

When he had ridden another quarter mile, his horse jumped sideways and he had to hang on as it backed into the brush. Harry levelled the rifle with one hand, searching the brush across the road.

'Kelsey?' he called.

Far off, a horse whickered and Harry's answered. Yet it remained nervous about something much closer, and he slipped down

215

and waited with the gun trained in the direction in which the horse was looking, ears up. The animal snorted and trembled, threw its head and tried to back.

'Logan,' a man said. Harry dived for the ground.

## CHAPTER TWENTY-FIVE

Harry lay on the road, waiting. The horse was pulling back, snorting in panic, but he held to the reins. While he waited his senses filtered every scrap of sound or shadow for meaning; but what he heard was a slow, steady sound of breathing, too heavy for a man, too light for a horse. It resembled snoring, and somehow made him think of the sounds that Laymon Russell made as he was coming to.

'Logan?' the voice said. 'Pete Canty . . . Over here.'

It was Canty's voice, no question of it. Canty hurt, or Canty foxy. He kept quiet. The horse was right there to give him away, but if Canty hadn't figured that out yet . . .

'Bleedin' to death,' Canty said in a horse, magnified whisper.

'That's too bad,' Harry said, risking it finally because time was leaking through his fingers like quicksilver. If she weren't here, he had to be riding to where she was.

'Gimme a hand,' said Canty in the brush.

'Where's Kelsey?' Harry took his eyes off the thicket where Canty lurked and ran them like a thief's fingers through the brush on either side. While he lay there, they might be pulling the drawstring.

'They've got her. Lute and the Mexican.'

'Where are they?'

'Headin' west. For your train.'

'With her?' scoffed Harry. 'You can do better than that.'

All the time the hoarse breathing went on, and Canty did not speak so much as he floated words and let the exhalations of his breath carry them away.

'Lute'll leave her some place,' he whispered.

'Are you shot?'

'Fingers shot off. Bleedin' to death.'

'So you'd like me to come in range. You put her in his hands, and now you want me to pose while you gun me down. I get the picture now. You're dying, for a fact, but you want company.'

He wriggled back into the brush, pulling the horse along. Then he rose cautiously and looked about. He swung up quickly, sure now of where he was going. Lute and Jacinto had the girl for a companion for the evening, like a drink after a big day's work. The next day's work would be trying to ambush him and Fiero.

'So long, Canty,' he said. 'Sorry I got to run.'

217

'Help me!' Canty said.

Harry rode a hundred yards, and then something like a rope yanked tight on him and he could go no farther. Five minutes might save a man's life, and could make little difference at the other end of this night.

He found the railroad man lying on his side fumbling with a sodden bandage. As he squatted beside him, Canty seemed only half aware of his presence. Harry pulled off Canty's heavy corduroy coat and flopped him on his back. He tore a strip from the coat, knotted the ends together and slipped the noose up his arm. His stomach drew up as he looked at the slack and bloody hand lying on the earth. The index finger had been shot away and the middle finger hung by a tendon. Thick and black, blood surged from the severed vessels with pitiless rhythm.

Harry's thumb dug into the big, helpless arm until he found the main blood vessel. The bleeding stopped as though a faucet had been turned off. As he arranged a pad of cloth under the tourniquet, he knew Canty was looking at him.

'Big country,' Canty said. 'More'n any one man can use sometimes.'

'Lots more. Can you hold this stick now? It'll keep the knot tight. I'll drag you into the road. They'll be along soon.'

Canty's hand took hold of the little crosspiece which acted like a lever to tighten

218

the tourniquet. Harry dragged him into the road.

'What is it about you?' Canty whispered. 'Stupid or religious? Same thing, I guess.'

'I guess. All I know is I'm in a hurry. Which way did they go?'

'Took off north into the foothills after they give up finding me. I crawled. They knew I had a gun.'

'And then they were going to double back and follow me, eh?' Harry stood there cleaning his hands with sand and trying to see into Lute Harper's mind.

'That's all I know. After we got Russell's valise and the girl, Lute took a shot at me out here. I rode a little way and fell off.' As Harry caught up his horse, Canty asked again, 'What is it about you? You could've let me die. You wouldn't have been a murderer. And nobody'd have known.'

'I'd have known. Tell me why that matters and you know more about me than I do,' Harry said.

'Good luck,' Canty said. His face seemed whiter than the alkali dust on the road. 'Double or nothing, Logan. Get Lute, and if I get back I'll clean your record till soap and water wouldn't have it. I don't figger you, but one thing you aren't is a killer.'

'There's lots like me,' Harry said. 'Most men are like me. But you don't find it out by putting a knife to their throats.'

219

He jogged on up the road until he found where the three remaining horses had left it to run towards the foothills.

He rode hard. They had a half hour's start on him, but that didn't mean much. They knew what a disorganized outfit the Russell train was, and might merely ride a few miles and settle down out of sight to enjoy their prizes. The only leverage he had on them was that they thought he was twenty miles away.

He loped when he could, studied trail sign when he had to, and kept his gun on full cock. The trail was climbing along the little mole burrow of mountains. It came to him that their horses must be about finished, for the hoof prints revealed that they were travelling fast. A window seemed to open to him in Lute Harper's sly mind, and his figuring was laid out like a diagram: Travel hard, get some rest and recreation, and wait for sunup to see whether there were pursuers and where they were. And travel accordingly.

He stopped to rest the horse. He could see even deeper into Lute's mind, but he was afraid to look. For with Canty dying, as Lute supposed, there was only Kelsey for a witness to what had happened tonight . . .

He kicked the horse, but it merely hunched and did not move. He threatened it with the stock of the rifle. Then he suddenly sniffed. Woodsmoke! He sat quietly, but he could hear only the loud thudding of his heart. The breeze blew gently in his face from the ridge just ahead. He had climbed high above the desert, so the smoke had to come from the ridge. Slipping from the saddle, he stood stiffly, pointing like a hound tasting the breeze. A voice came faintly, a voice hardly louder than the breeze hissing through the Spanish bayonet, a Mexican voice singing slow and sad. Harry advanced, trying the ground with his boot before he set it down. He climbed the slope with the patient, deadly care of a cat.

A fragrance of coffee mingled with that of the smoke. A voice nasal with the accents of Missouri complained, 'You call that singing, boy? You listen to this.' A throat was cleared, and a voice began, ' "Say, have you heard 'bout Sweet Betsey from Pike, crossed the—crossed the—" What the hell'd she cross, Kels?'

There was no reply, and Lute's voice rapped, 'I asked you something.'

Presently he resumed, ' "—Crossed the wide prairie with her lover, Ike—" Git away from that valise, greaser,' he interrupted himself coldly.

Now Harry was quite close. He saw the firelight tipping the desert shrubs above him. The camp was in a little hollow just across the crest. He moved like an infantryman, the stock of the gun against his ribs.

'What's the matter, *amigo?*' asked Jacinto reproachfully. 'You afraid I'm going to steal it?'

221

'Nothin' in it but dirty socks,' said Luther, 'but I'm kind of partial to dirty socks. Honey baby,' he complained in a new voice, 'you keep movin' away from me, like I ain't so bad, am I? Give me a little chance and I bet you'll say I'm pretty good.'

'Leave—me—alone.' It was the voice of a girl who had wept until her voice was husky from weeping.

'Oh, now, don't say that like you mean it. If I thought you and me could get along, it might make a lot of difference about things. I brought you along some clothes, didn't I? So I must be a pretty thoughtful feller.'

Down the hill, Harry's horse whickered. A short distance across the ridge, other horses answered. 'Hey, what the hell?' said Lute. He came scrambling up.

Harry sprinted hard until the fire and the little camp appeared in a scoop of the hillside below him. Jacinto was lolling on one elbow, but as Harry watched he dropped the tin cup he held and picked up a revolver. He was staring at the man above them with a waxy expression of astonishment. On the edge of the firelight, Lute, holding a Colt, was pulling a girl in a dressing sacque against him.

Harry pressed his cheek against the gun stock. He heard Kelsey scream just as the rifle blasted its bolt of smoke and thunder down the slope. He ducked away, cocking the gun. The flash of the powder remained in his eyes like a

222

stain. He waited and heard Lute's shot come up at him with a massive roar. A bullet hit the ground between his feet. The report was a physical thing that jolted him back. He heard Lute struggling with the girl, heard him swearing in a tight, furious voice and Kelsey screaming at him as she fought.

Harry's eyes cleared. He saw her break away and run a few yards and fall, as Lute, his face thin and yellow, swung the Colt after her. Harry fired without aiming, slung the empty rifle at him and ran down the slope. Lute was still standing there in the firelight, and Kelsey lying on the ground a few strides from him. Harry began firing his Colt. Lute reeled back and collapsed in a stiff clump of brush. His revolver hung loosely by the finger through the trigger guard. Harry fired until the Colt was empty. The gun hanging, then, he looked for Kelsey. She lay still. The gun dropped from his hand as he moved forward.

'Kelsey . . .'

She raised her head as he knelt beside her. She put out her hand to him and Harry caught her from the ground and rocked her in his arms.

'Take me away from here,' she whispered. 'I don't want to know . . .'

As he carried her up the hill, she said, 'I knew you'd come.'

'I was twenty miles away, and you knew it?'

'Once you were a thousand miles away and

you came. I was going back tomorrow. If I had to walk.'

'You aren't going to walk. You're going to ride up there beside me after this. Where a stage man's girl belongs.'

'Where I belong,' she whispered.

*     *     *

There was an American barber in Albuquerque, a very old man with a face like onion skin and a yellow toupee. Outside his shop Harry saw Fiero's horse when the remnants of the Russell party returned the following afternoon. He had brought them back so that Russell might recover properly, Canty might be treated, and a new guide hired. The mail agent found rooms for everyone and Harry saw Kelsey settled for the night. In the morning they would start back to the camp.

Fiero had been trimmed and shaved and now he was soaking in the big wooden barrel behind a curtain in the rear. Harry talked with him while the old man's shears whispered about his ear.

'Told you I was for California,' he reminded him.

'Yep,' said Fiero cheerfully. There was a luxurious sloshing sound of soapy water.

'Why'd you come in town?'

'Get a bath and a haircut.'

'I thought you were worried about me.'

'Well, that too.'

'I hope you warned Hilario to keep a lookout for fires. That Judith girl's an odd one. Of course she's got an interest in the coaches now. That might make a difference.'

'I talked to her about it.' Fiero sounded complacent. 'Anyway, she'll sleep from sundown to sunup. She was pretty tired today.'

'How's that?'

Fiero slopped water again. 'We went for a walk last night. Must've walked twenty miles. I thought it was a good way to keep her out of mischief.'

Harry settled back in the chair, feeling relaxed about something which had disturbed him very much before. 'You did, eh?'

'*And* she didn't burn any stages. She's a funny one, that girl. I guess she's kind of *loco*, but she's got a good head, too. Some ways she thinks like a horse-trader. Other ways she's all woman.'

'All woman's a good way for a woman to be,' said Harry.

'That says it,' agreed Fiero.

We hope you have enjoyed this Large Print book. Other Chivers Press or G.K. Hall & Co. Large Print books are available at your library or directly from the publishers.

For more information about current and forthcoming titles, please call or write, without obligation, to:

Chivers Press Limited
Windsor Bridge Road
Bath BA2 3AX
England
Tel. (01225) 335336

OR

G.K. Hall & Co.
P.O. Box 159
Thorndike, Maine 04986
USA
Tel. (800) 223-2336

All our Large Print titles are designed for easy reading, and all our books are made to last.